MB

W9-AXC-041

"I'm really sorry but we're about to close," Lillie said.

"The way my day's been going, that figures." He shook her hand, then glanced at his fingers. She'd inadvertantly offered a hand that still had gravy on it.

"Sorry. We were cleaning up."

"That's okay. If I was really hungry, I suppose I could just lick my fingers." As he wiped his hands on a napkin, he said, "I'm James Warner."

"Lillie Delaney."

He grabbed her hand and pumped it eagerly, gravy and all. "So *you're* Lillie. I'm glad to finally meet you. Your grandmother has nothing but good things to say about you."

"She's prejudiced," Lillie said, wishing Gram had talked about the new preacher.

He smiled and Lillie's blush deepened. His leather jacket made him look like a cross between a member of a biker gang and a WWII fighter pilot. No wonder the church was running out of room. The congregation had to be overflowing with eligible women now that James was its pastor.

VALERIE HANSEN

was thirty when she awoke to the presence of the Lord in her life and turned to Jesus. In the years that followed she worked with young children, both in church and secular environments. She also raised a family of her own and played foster mother to a wide assortment of furred and feathered critters.

Married to her high school sweetheart since age seventeen, she now lives in an old farmhouse she and her husband renovated with their own hands. She loves to hike the wooded hills behind the house and reflect on the marvelous turn her life has taken. Not only is she privileged to reside among the loving, accepting folks in the breathtakingly beautiful Ozark mountains of Arkansas, she also gets to share her personal faith by telling the stories of her heart for Steeple Hill's Love Inspired line.

Life doesn't get much better than that!

A Treasure
of the Heart
Valerie Hansen

Steeple
Hill®

Published by Steeple Hill Books™

If you purchased this book without a cover you should be aware that this book is stolen property. It was reported as "unsold and destroyed" to the publisher, and neither the author nor the publisher has received any payment for this "stripped book."

STEEPLE HILL BOOKS

Steeple Hill®

ISBN-13: 978-0-373-81327-8
ISBN-10:   0-373-81327-9

A TREASURE OF THE HEART

Copyright © 2007 by Valerie Whisenand

All rights reserved. Except for use in any review, the reproduction or utilization of this work in whole or in part in any form by any electronic, mechanical or other means, now known or hereafter invented, including xerography, photocopying and recording, or in any information storage or retrieval system, is forbidden without the written permission of the editorial office, Steeple Hill Books, 233 Broadway, New York, NY 10279 U.S.A.

This is a work of fiction. Names, characters, places and incidents are either the product of the author's imagination or are used fictitiously, and any resemblance to actual persons, living or dead, business establishments, events or locales is entirely coincidental.

This edition published by arrangement with Steeple Hill Books.

® and TM are trademarks of Steeple Hill Books, used under license. Trademarks indicated with ® are registered in the United States Patent and Trademark Office, the Canadian Trade Marks Office and in other countries.

www.SteepleHill.com

Printed in U.S.A.

If it is possible, as much as it depends on you,
live peaceably with all men.

—*Romans* 12:18

Many thanks to Bert and Troy for explaining all the ins and outs of running a small restaurant. Not only are they nice people, their restaurant offers the best-tasting, home-style meals for miles around. And thanks to Joe for taking me there to eat so often!

Chapter One

There were times when days, even weeks, passed without a thought of her past. Then, some little thing would jog Lillie Delaney's memory and her mind would flit back to Gumption, Arkansas, and the idyllic life she'd once led as a child growing up in the foothills of the Ozark Mountains.

Today, the trigger was a scrap of paper resembling a dry leaf being carried along by the rainwater in a curbside gutter. As Lillie watched, her make-believe leaf became a homemade boat, the gutter a meandering creek and Lillie a seven-year-old seeing her tiny craft sail out of reach.

"Catch it!"

"You catch it. It's your boat."

Squealing, Lillie had jumped feetfirst into the stream, slipped on a mossy rock and landed on her back pockets in the icy water while a neighbor boy and his sister had giggled over her plight. She'd been sure she'd be scolded for coming home all wet that day. Instead, Gram had found the incident so funny she'd hugged little Lillie and they'd laughed together until tears had run down their cheeks.

Lillie sighed. Breathed deeply. Brought herself back to the present and hurried across the busy city street as the traffic light changed in her favor. There was something refreshing about the air after a storm, even though the wind off Lake Michigan was cutting through her heavy coat and chilling her to the bone. Here in Chicago she welcomed showers because they cleansed the atmosphere and left behind a temporary respite from the pollution of the bustling city.

Back home in Gumption, the rain always gave the air a heavy sweetness as it nourished the forested hills. This time of year, redbud trees would be finishing their display and dogwoods would be spreading creamy-white four-petal flowers in the dappled shade of the soon-to-leaf-out oaks. Yellowish-green buds would make the forest shimmer in the rain's aftermath, glistening with the promise of the coming canopy; a roof of coolness beneath the arching azure of a cloudless Southern summer sky.

Shivering, Lillie pushed her way through the revolving door into the imposing stone office building where she'd worked for years. Her heels clacked against the polished marble floor of the crowded lobby. Concerned about the time, she hurried to the elevator and pushed the up button again, even though it was already lit. Slick streets had made her late, not that anyone upstairs would believe that excuse. No one employed there had a passion for his or her job. They simply reported in the morning, put in their required hours behind a desk and went home as soon as possible. That blasé attitude had been hard for Lillie to understand until she'd spent a few months walking in their shoes—or rather, sitting in their desk chairs.

She huffed as she stepped onto the elevator. *Months, nothing.* She'd been stuck in basically the same job for much longer than that and she was now at the top step in her department. Granted, somebody had to manage the clerks who processed medical insurance records and ordered the authorized payments but if there was a more boring job in the world she couldn't imagine what it could be.

Three men wearing raincoats and a middle-aged woman carrying a folded, dripping umbrella followed her onto the already crowded elevator. Pressed into a rear corner, Lillie felt nearly as uncomfortable as she had the time she and her girlfriends had crammed together into the janitor's closet at school, meaning to scare him, and had panicked and nearly suffocated when they'd accidentally locked themselves in. To this day, being in total darkness gave her the willies.

There was no accident involved with her present position, however. She'd come to the city to seek excitement and glamour and had found, instead, boredom and dingy sameness masquerading as job security.

Part of her loneliness was admittedly her own fault. Though she did attend church occasionally, she had never become fully involved in the kind of social life that would bring her into contact with many like-minded people. A few friends from work had invited her to go clubbing with them, years ago, and she had given it a try. In retrospect, she realized they'd meant well but she'd felt about as comfortable in that situation as a newly landed catfish flopping around in the bottom of a fishing boat. Both were clearly out of their element.

The mental picture made her smile. As she removed her scarf and fluffed her shoulder-length light brown hair, she glanced at the woman with the umbrella, wishing she could share her good humor with someone. She was rewarded with a scowl.

"If I wanted to live in a city, I should have gone farther south instead of coming this direction," Lillie mumbled.

"Beg your pardon?"

Lillie's smile waned, her blue eyes misty. "Never mind. I was just talking to myself." The elevator stopped at Lillie's floor. "Excuse me, please." She edged toward the open door, bumping shoulders with others in spite of efforts to take care. "Excuse me. I have to get off."

Someone held the doors long enough for her to exit. They slid closed behind her with a hiss while her last words echoed repeatedly in her mind. *I have to get off. I have to get off.*

Instead of rushing to her office, she stood in the cavernous hallway, blinking as reality seeped in. Her heart was the only part of her that was still racing and it was galloping laps around her muddled brain. What was she doing here? Why hadn't she admitted her mistakes long ago, gotten off this figurative treadmill and headed home where she belonged?

The answer was pride. Except for the occasional visit when she had lauded city life as if all her dreams had come true, pride had kept her from going back to Gumption. And pride could keep her locked in the same dead-end job for literally a lifetime if she let it.

She didn't want to run home to Grandma Darla Sue and admit defeat but she didn't want to waste what remained of her life, either. There had to be more to a worthwhile existence than she'd found so far. Maybe she was expecting too much. Then again, maybe she'd once lived in the perfect place and had been too dense or stubborn to recognize it.

Lillie squared her shoulders and strode toward her office. There was only one way to find out. She was going to muster her courage, give the two weeks' notice and head for the only place that had ever felt truly like home.

To Lillie's surprise her superiors had decided that two weeks' notice was unnecessary, had accepted her resignation and had told her she was free to leave immediately.

So much for being indispensable!

She'd said a somber if relieved goodbye to coworkers in nearby cubicles and had been on her way home to her apartment to start packing within the hour.

Some of her friends had wanted to throw a going-away party but Lillie talked them out of it by promising to return for her stored furniture and let them have a get-together then, if they still wanted to.

Two days later she was on the road, driving south in a mental haze and wondering what had come over her. There she was, too close to thirty-five for comfort, unemployed and heading for the only place that had ever felt like a real home. The notion of plunking herself back into Grandma Darla Sue's and Grandpa Max's lives and making their house her home again, the way she had been forced to as a lonely child, gave her colder chills than the gales off Lake Michigan.

If she used up her savings before she found another job, there was always the value of her furniture to fall back on, she reasoned. She knew her friends would sell it for her and send her the money if she them her to. At least she knew they would if they still lived there. If there was one thing Lillie had learned about life in the big city it was how fast everything could change.

All she really wanted was to reclaim the peace she'd so foolishly left behind when she'd moved North. If that meant she had to bite the bullet and spend a few weeks staying with her grandparents till she got back on her feet, then she would. She figured, as long as she explained to stubborn, reclusive Grandpa Max that she didn't intend to stay for more than a few weeks he wouldn't pitch too big a fit about sharing his peace and quiet with

her again. Now that she was older and hope-
fully wiser, she could see that one of the
reasons she and Max had butted heads was
that they were so much alike under the
surface.

Passing through Serenity and entering
Gumption on Highway 62, Lillie noticed
little difference since her last brief visit, at
least not on the surface. The courthouse in
the town square and its bordering stores were
still the center of activity. Tall, silvery-leafed
poplars had replaced some of the old maples
on the courthouse lawn and the streets looked
narrower than they had when she was a child,
but other than that the place seemed pretty
much the same. The entire area was sort of
stuck in a time warp, which in her case was
exactly what she craved.

She sighed. It was truly good to be home.
She just hoped her favorite resident wasn't
going to be too disappointed in her for
quitting a steady job. The work ethic was
strong in Darla Sue Howell. She'd kept her
little café going in spite of Max's lack of en-
couragement and had made room for Lillie
when her parents' marriage had self-de-
structed and the ensuing divorce had sent

her mother into a bottomless pit of self-pity. Lillie loved Darla Sue more than anything in the world and there wasn't anyone she wanted more to please.

Eager to surprise her grandmother at work, she parked her blue sedan in one of the spaces surrounding the courthouse, grabbed her purse and a sweater and slid out, resisting the urge to lock the car door. Folks in Gumption trusted their neighbors. If she were to lock the door she'd immediately demonstrate that she no longer fit into this lifestyle. Better to chance losing whatever inconsequential items she'd left piled on the car seats than to be immediately ostracized as an outsider.

Smiling and feeling amazingly free, she slipped the sweater on and crossed the street to the café. The sign over the door had once read, Darla's Deli, but the red paint on the smaller letters had faded until all that remained were the two capital *D*s. For as long as Lillie could recall, the place had simply been "DD's" and so it still was.

During her Christmas visit she'd offered to climb up and repaint the sign in spite of the freezing temperature but her grandmother wouldn't hear of it. Darla Sue had said, if folks didn't know who she was or what she served in the café, they didn't need to be coming in, anyway. Since business had always been good enough to keep her busy and employ a small staff, Lillie had had to agree.

The aroma of fresh-brewed coffee and homemade biscuits filled Lillie's senses as she pushed open the restaurant door. Original decor that had remained unchanged for so long that it was now referred to as *retro* prompted a rush of nostalgia. Framed pictures of old film stars and even older cars lined the walls. Paper place mats and packets of silverware rolled inside white napkins graced the tables and a vase with a single silk flower was carefully centered behind each set of salt-and-pepper shakers. Come summer, when Darla Sue's garden was in full bloom, the flowers in those milk-glass vases would be real.

Lillie sighed. Coming here was so much like stepping back into childhood she immediately craved a warm oatmeal-raisin cookie and an equally warm hug from her darling grandmother.

Pausing at the entrance to scan the sparse crowd, she garnered a few amiable nods but saw no one she recognized outright. That was the way it had been the last few times she'd visited. Many of the old-timers who'd known her as a child had either passed away or moved to condos in Florida, bless their hearts. Every trip home had made her feel less and less a part of life in Gumption. Perhaps that was one of the reasons she'd felt such a strong pull to return for good.

She crossed the room, heels clicking on the black-and-white checkerboard-tiled floor and peeked in the kitchen door, fully expecting to find her grandmother standing at the grill, wearing a chef's apron and wielding a spatula.

Instead, she saw a stranger. The middle-aged woman's washed-out blond hair was pulled back by a rolled blue bandanna and escaped curls were plastered to her forehead and neck by perspiration.

The woman glowered. "What's the matter? Didn't like your eggs?"

"No. I haven't even eaten." Lillie recovered from her astonishment and extended her hand. "I'm Lillie Delaney, Darla Sue's granddaughter. I'm afraid we haven't met."

"I'm Rosie," the woman said without shaking her hand. "Do you cook?"

"A little. Why?"

Rosie whipped off the scarf and threw it aside, then untied her apron strings. "Because you can have this job. I quit."

Lillie instinctively backed up. When she'd wished for gainful employment she hadn't meant anything like this. Cooking had never been her forte. Eating, maybe. Preparing a meal with more than three ingredients, no way.

"Hold it," she said, trying to sound amiable in the face of the woman's obvious distress. "I know exactly how you feel but I didn't come here to take your job, Rosie. I'm just looking for my grandmother. Please stay."

She sighed. "Okay. But I warn you, one more complaint from some good old boy who just assumes I'll know how he wants his stupid food cooked, or what he hates, and I'm out of here."

"Gram is pretty good at remembering that kind of detail," Lillie said. "Is she taking the day off?"

"More like the month," the harried cook answered. "I was supposed to be her assistant. She said she was going to teach me the ropes. We got started fine the first day. Then she stepped out to get a few things at the market and never came back to work."

"She isn't missing, is she?!"

"No, no. According to old Rayford Evans she just wandered on home. He was havin' coffee in here with the other retired farmers, just like he always does, and that waitress, Helen, sent him over to her house to check. He said Darla Sue was bakin' cookies when he got there and actin' as if everything was hunky-dory."

"How long ago was that?"

"Only about two weeks, I guess. Seems like years."

"I'm so sorry," Lillie said. "We'll make arrangements to get you some help, I promise." She glanced over her shoulder as the back door slammed. "Helen! Thank goodness. I was afraid poor Rosie was stuck here all by herself."

Helen engulfed Lillie in a smothering, motherly embrace. Lillie couldn't help noticing that the portly woman's clothing and hair smelled of vanilla, bacon and cigarettes. Gram used to smell like that, too, except without the nicotine. The familiar aromas tugged at Lillie's heart.

"I just went to dump the trash and grab a quick smoke," Helen said. "It's been crazy here lately. Miss Darla's gone off the deep end, business is terrible and somebody's been tryin' to run off the new preacher at the Front Porch Christian Church. I was just talkin' to Rayford and a few of the other regular customers about it."

Lillie blinked, disbelieving. Storytelling had long ago risen to the status of a fine art in Gumption and she didn't presume for a second that the rumors were true. Still, if Darla Sue was having problems, as Rosie had intimated, maybe there was a grain of truth to Helen's statement.

"What's wrong with Gram?" Lillie asked.

"It's a long story. You plannin' on stayin' a spell? Miss Darla can use a shoulder to cry on right about now."

"Business is really bad?"

"The pits." Helen glanced at the morose cook. "It's not Rosie's fault. She's doin' her best. So am I. It's just that Miss Darla did all the ordering and we're not keeping up very well without her."

"Why hasn't she been coming in?"

The waitress tsk-tsked and shook her head. "That's for her to say. Personally, I think she had a nervous breakdown or some such thing."

"Oh, dear." The last part of Helen's earlier revelation was echoing in the back of Lillie's mind. "What does that have to do with a new preacher at Gram's church?"

"Nothin'. That's a whole other story," the waitress said. "Tell you what. Why don't you go see about Darla Sue first. The gossip about the preacher'll wait."

"Are you positive there were attempts to get rid of the man? I mean, things like that just don't happen around here."

"Looks like they do now. The minute Brother James started talkin' about buildin' a new church, strange things started happening."

Lillie knew how the locals hated change but she couldn't picture them resorting to violence to stop it. "Maybe the guy is just accident-prone."

Helen snorted. "If he is, it's rubbed off on the church, too."

Although Lillie was intrigued, she knew

her primary duty was to Darla Sue. "Okay. Tell you what. I'll go say hello to Gram like you suggested and look over the situation at home. When I get back, I want to hear the rest of your story about the new preacher."

"Take your time," Rosie said with a stifled yawn. "This is Friday so we're open for supper, too. We'll be stuck here till after nine, like it or not."

Lillie was almost to the door when she heard Rosie add, "And I *don't* like it. Man, I hate this job."

The echo of her own career woes gave Lillie the shivers. Even paradise had its share of problems, didn't it?

The engine of the massive motorcycle didn't hum or buzz like those little imported bikes; it thumped in a galloping cadence reminiscent of the old single-cylinder gas engines that had once powered farm machinery and primitive factories from Maine to California.

Pastor James Warner often thought of the sound as the heartbeat of the beast he rode. Though he'd given in to the deacons' urging that he wear a helmet, he was not about to give up the independence he'd found riding such a formidable machine. The Harley was the only thing he'd salvaged after his former life had fallen apart around him and he intended to hang on to it. After all, it wasn't as if he had to drive a car in order to ferry family members. Except for God, he was essentially alone. And that was the way he liked it.

Snug in his black leather bomber jacket, he reveled in the sensation of the cool wind on his face, the unfettered freedom of movement, the way the motorcycle seemed to become an extension of his personality. Riding was more than an escape. It put him in tune with nature and that somehow brought him closer to God.

Funny, he thought. There had been times lately when he'd felt so blessed he'd wondered if he'd accidentally wandered into someone else's life!

He began to grin. Members of his flock had made no secret of their worries that riding the bike would bring him face-to-face with his Maker before his time. He respectfully disagreed. Either he was in God's hands all the time, or he never was. Psalm

139 said he was "fearfully and wonderfully made" and that God had known him even before he was born, so how could it be otherwise?

He shifted, banked and cornered, passing DD's café. One of his recent disappointments was his inability to get through to Mrs. Howell. But he wasn't going to give up. No, sir. Darla Sue Howell had once been a driving force in his church and she would be again. All he had to do was figure out how to inspire her and draw her back into the fold.

James grimaced. The last time he'd paid her a call he'd had to talk to her through a closed door. He knew she'd heard the Harley pull into her driveway because she'd slammed the front door practically in his face.

"It's me, Mrs. Howell," he'd called pleasantly, helmet in hand so she could see his face if she chose to peek out. "Brother James Warner."

"I know who it is," Darla Sue had shouted from inside the house. "Go away."

"I'd have called first but your phone is out of order."

"No, it's not. I took it off the hook."

"Are you feeling all right?"

"Right as rain," she'd answered.

"We miss you at church. It's not the same without you sitting in the front pew, keeping an eye on things."

"Bah. Nobody misses me."

"I do."

"You're supposed to miss me. It's your job," she'd snapped.

James had been at a temporary loss for words. She was right, yet there was much more to it than that. He did care. Deeply. It was one of the drawbacks of being a minister of the gospel. When the people in his congregation hurt, he hurt for them. Then again, when they were joyful he shared in that, too.

Sometimes, when he caught himself wishing there was more to be happy about, he'd recall the life he'd led before he'd come to Gumption. There was no comparison.

His only regret, at this point, was that it had taken him so long to find the right path and start to walk it. He had a lot of catching up to do and he was looking forward to meeting those challenges.

Chapter Two

Lillie's grandparents' home was one of those brick places that had started out as a simple rectangle and had grown into a sprawling megalith over the years. Darla Sue and Max had raised their own five children, seen them off to college or married or both, and then taken in Lillie, their only granddaughter. It had been clear at the time that Max had considered his child-rearing days completed. He had acted far from eager to welcome another youngster into the house but Gram had treated Lillie as if she were the only bright star in the sky.

Back then, Lillie had accepted that love as her due, but in retrospect she could see what a strain her presence must have placed on her grandparents and their marriage. To Darla Sue's credit, she had never complained or said she wished she was free of the added responsibility of a child.

Max's pickup truck wasn't in the drive when Lillie arrived but Darla Sue's car was. Parking next to a bed of nodding yellow daffodils, Lillie got out and climbed the wooden porch steps leading to the back door. Gram's latest pair of tattered gardening sneakers had been kicked off and left beside the mat, just as they had been in years past. The familiar sight tugged at Lillie's memories and transported her back to her childhood. What small feet Gram had. Funny how she'd never noticed that before.

Smiling and sighing, she knocked on the back screen door, got no answer and let herself in with a cheery "Hello? Gram? It's me!"

The kitchen hadn't changed in years, either. It was still typical of the 1950s, with homemade cabinets of cedar and a floor covered with worn linoleum instead of more modern vinyl. In one end of the kitchen sat the familiar chrome-and-red-plastic dinette set.

Darla Sue called out her answer from the

other room as if Lillie hadn't been away at all, let alone living in Illinois for years. "Hoo-whee! Lillie, honey. Come on in! You're just in time. I was fixin' to make your favorite, fried cherry pies."

Uh-oh, she thought. *Southern comfort food. The answer to any kind of stress. Run for your life Mr. Bathroom Scale, here comes the new, super-sized Lillie Delaney.*

"Thanks, Gram. Sounds good," she replied, vowing to limit her intake at all costs. After thirty she'd found that the slightest dab of extra food added to her hips, seemingly overnight, and a fried pie was considerably more than a dab. It was more like a semitruckload.

When Darla Sue appeared in the doorway from the living room, Lillie's blue eyes widened in surprise. Most of Gram's quirks were familiar to her. This latest one, however, was brand new. And it was such doozy she almost laughed out loud.

Although Darla Sue was fully dressed, her curly hair was tucked neatly beneath a pink bouffant shower cap.

"What?" The old woman scowled in response to Lillie's evident amusement.

"I was just noticing your…um…hat."

"What about it?"

Lillie struggled to keep a straight face and failed. "Did you forget to take it off after you showered?"

"Nope."

"But, you're wearing…"

"I know what I'm wearing, girl. I put it on, didn't I?" She started into the kitchen. "It's chilly today. I could use a cup of tea."

"Okay. Let's sit and talk a bit. I want to ask you why you haven't been going to work."

The disgusted look on her grandmother's face made Lillie's grin spread. Knowing this spry elderly enigma, she'd beat around the bush for a while, then eventually tell all. It was waiting for her to get to the point that was always the most frustrating.

The older woman displaced a snoozing yellow cat and settled herself in one of the chrome-and-red plastic dinette chairs. She watched quietly while Lillie filled the copper tea kettle, set it on the front burner and lit the antiquated stove with a match before she said, "It's all that Wanda's fault."

"What is? The cap, or not going to work?"

"Both." Darla Sue tapped the pink plastic

cap for emphasis. "I couldn't find my mama's babushka. You used to play with it when you were little. Remember? It was paisley, with a brown border."

"I do remember that old scarf. Whenever I'd put it on you used to say I looked just like the pictures of Great Great-Grandma Emily when she was an immigrant."

"That's the one. Anyhow, it's missing."

One of Lillie's eyebrows arched. "Okay. What does that have to do with staying home from work?"

"Everything. And don't look at me like that, girl. I'm not daft."

"Hey, I never said you were. But you are confusing sometimes. Maybe we'd better concentrate on one problem at a time. Tell me about Wanda first."

"Okay. She got a newfangled phone. One of those little ones that takes pictures and shows you who you're talking to."

Lillie fetched two mugs and put a tea bag in each before bringing them to the table while she waited for the water to boil. "What does that have to do with the scarf?"

"I'm getting around to it," the elderly woman grumbled. "The director at the Senior

Center has one of those phones, too, a little blue one. I stopped by there on my way to the market the other day and had a chance to try it out."

"And you called Wanda? Gram, that's long distance."

"I know. But I couldn't think of anybody else who had one of those stupid camera things and the director said it was all right."

Lillie nodded, hoping to convey empathy. "Go on."

"I was all set to have a fine set-down visit with Wanda, just like we used to do before she moved so far away. Might have, too, if it hadn't been for that telephone. Wanda took one look at the snapshot of me on her phone and busted out laughing."

"Why?"

Darla Sue's thin fingers grasped the cap and pulled it off. "'Cause of this."

"Your hair?" Lillie blinked, more puzzled than ever.

"Yep. When Wanda finally stopped cackling like a hen on a nest of fresh eggs, she said I looked like a skunk."

"Oh, dear." Lillie had to bite her lip to

keep from agreeing. "You're letting your hair grow out?"

"It would appear so."

"And that's why you haven't been at the café?"

"Bingo. I always did think you were a smart cookie."

Lillie was frowning. "I still don't see the problem. I mean, I can understand why you'd be miffed at Wanda for laughing at you but you could still go in to work. There's not a thing wrong with gray hair. I don't know why you dyed it for so many years, anyway. If you want to go gray, why don't you just have the dyed part stripped of color?"

Darla Sue had a faraway look in her eyes, as if her mind was elsewhere, and she didn't respond to Lillie's sensible suggestion. Instead, she said, "Max didn't cotton to gray, you know. That's why I kept it dark. For him. Now that he's gone, I decided it was time to be myself for a change."

Lillie froze. Was Gram saying what Lillie thought she was saying? "Grandpa Max is dead?" She gently took the old woman's hands. "I'm so sorry. Why didn't you tell me?"

"Not dead, you ninny." Darla Sue pulled away with a cynical grimace. "Gone. Took off for Florida with one of them fancy single floozies from the retirement center." She sighed. "I suppose he'll be back. He always comes home eventually."

"Whoa." The teakettle began to whistle in the background. Lillie ignored it. "Always? Grandpa's done this kind of thing before?"

"Three times, more's the pity. You'd think a man his age would be over this silliness by now, wouldn't you?"

Lillie was nearly speechless. "But…"

"The first time he left me was when your mama was little. That was the scariest, me being alone and all. The second time it happened was before you were born."

"Why didn't you ever tell me?"

"Things were hard enough between you and Max, thanks to his stubborn, selfish nature. I always took him back and forgave him, so there was no need to keep bringin' up the past."

"That's unbelievable."

"Not to me it isn't." Her chin jutted out stubbornly. She smashed the shower cap back onto her head and poked stray curls beneath the elastic band with jabs of her thin, quick fingers. "That tea water's boilin'. You wanna go get it or shall I?"

It was hours later before Lillie had a chance to steal away and place a private call to her mother, Sandra, in Harrison.

As soon as Sandra said hello, Lillie followed with "Why didn't you tell me about Grandpa Max?"

"Oh, dear. Mom's been blabbing, hasn't she?"

"She said he ran off with a floozy. I can't believe he's such a stinker."

"He isn't. He's just a man. They can't help it."

"Phooey. Daddy wasn't like that." The dead silence on the other end of the line made Lillie's heart sink. "Mom?"

"Your father was a good man—most of the time. And he was a wonderful provider. I'm just sorry you had to see us go through that awful divorce."

"Daddy cheated?" Lillie felt as if her childhood had just imploded. No wonder her mother had suffered so much. She'd known the whole sordid truth. And now Lillie did. The reputation of the man she had loved and admired most while growing up had just been destroyed.

Head spinning, she barely heard her mother asking, "So, how was the trip back to Gumption? How's Mom?" There was a short pause. "Lillie? Are you still there?"

"I'm here," she managed to say. Once she started to speak, casual conversation seemed to get easier. "Gram's fine, if you don't count the shower cap she insists on wearing all the time to cover her gray roots."

"I told her to get a haircut weeks ago. See if you can talk her into it while you're there, will you?"

"Sure."

"Honey? Are you okay?"

"Me? Of course. Why wouldn't I be? I've just learned the truth about something that affected my entire childhood. That one fact finally answered the thousands of questions I've been asking myself for years. Trouble is, I don't like those answers one bit."

"I'm so sorry, honey. I just assumed you'd figured it out a long time ago, what with the way gossip travels in a small town like Gumption."

"Well, 'Ask and you shall receive,'" Lillie replied. She couldn't blame God or anybody else if she'd gotten exactly the kind of answers she'd asked for, could she? And it did explain so much.

Suppose her mother had been the kind of resilient woman Darla Sue was? Suppose she'd chosen to forgive and keep their family together instead of divorcing Dad?

Then I wouldn't have come to live with Gram and we'd probably never have been this close, Lillie realized with a start. *Think what I'd have missed!*

That conclusion made her smile in spite of everything. It looked as if maybe the good Lord did know what He was doing after all.

Lillie didn't get back to DD's till almost closing time. A skinny, acne-pocked kid she'd never met was stacking dishes in the utility sink when she popped in the back door. He glanced up briefly but didn't seem nearly as surprised to see her as she was to see him.

She gave him a passing "Hi," hung her jacket on a hook in the back room and went to find Helen. The faithful waitress was busing the last of the tables along the outside wall so Lillie pitched in to help.

"Thanks," Helen said as they carried stacks of dirty plates to the cart and scraped off the garbage before sorting the dishes, silverware and plastic tumblers into separate bins. "How was the boss lady?"

"Fine, if you don't mind seeing her in a shower cap all the time."

Helen laughed. "That's a new one."

"It's her hair," Lillie said with a smile. "One of her friends teased her about letting the gray grow out and she refuses to let anyone else see it till it's long enough to have all the dyed parts cut off. That's why she's been staying home."

"Makes perfect sense to me. I used to be a redhead, back when I thought it mattered. Now, who cares? Plain brown is fine at my age. Besides, all the good men are taken."

"I think you look nice."

"Thanks. Speaking of good men, how's *your* love life? Didn't I hear you were thinkin' of gettin' married a while back?"

"That's old news," Lillie said flatly. "It didn't work out."

"Well, you always have your career," Helen offered.

That smarted. "Not exactly. I quit my job."

"Uh-oh. Does Darla Sue know?"

"No. I didn't see any reason to mention it right away, considering all the other problems she's facing. I'll find work locally before I tell her."

From the kitchen came a shouted "You can have my job!"

Lillie laughed. "Sorry, Rosie, I'm a terrible cook. You're stuck, at least till I can convince Gram her hair doesn't look funny."

She made another trip to the dirty-dish cart. It had been years since she'd helped out in the café like this and she wasn't as adroit as she'd once been. When she finished scooping refuse and turned, she realized she was sporting a smear of the restaurant's trademark red-eye gravy across the front of her formerly pristine pink blouse.

"Oh, yuck." She grabbed a napkin and started dabbing at the stain, knowing the grease mark was probably already permanent.

The bell over the front door tinkled. She looked up from her cleaning project and saw a man entering. His leather jacket made him look like a cross between a member of a biker gang and a handsome, intriguing World War II fighter pilot. She'd opened her mouth to tell him politely that they were about to close when Helen elbowed her.

"That's him," the waitress hissed. "The preacher I told you about. His name's James something-or-other." She paused and sighed. "Poor man. He looks really beat."

"And hungry," Lillie added, noting the little lines of stress creasing his forehead above dark eyebrows and warm brown eyes. "I suppose it would be neighborly to feed him, even this late."

"Not unless you want Rosie to pitch a fit," Helen gibed. "She's more than ready to go home."

Lillie figured it was probably better to avoid conflict so she stuck out her right hand and went to head off the hungry preacher before he could sit down.

"Hello. I'm really sorry but we're about to close," she said, hoping the wash rag she was holding in front of her hid the soiled spot on her blouse.

"The way my day's been going, that figures." He shook her hand, then glanced at his fingers, which caused her to do the same.

In her haste to stop him she'd inadvertently offered a hand that still had gravy on it.

Her cheeks warmed. "Oops. Sorry. We were cleaning up."

"That's okay. If I was really hungry I suppose I could just lick my fingers."

In the background, Helen giggled. The dirty look Lillie gave her only made her laugh more.

"I'm James Warner," the man said as he wiped his hands on a paper napkin he'd snagged from one of the tables.

"Lillie Delaney." She was about to explain her relationship to Darla Sue when he grabbed her hand a second time and pumped it eagerly, gravy and all. "So, you're Lillie. I am glad to finally meet you. Your grandmother has nothing but good things to say about you."

"She's prejudiced," Lillie said, feeling her cheeks reddening more. She wished Gram had talked about the new preacher so she'd know more about him than Helen's notion that some folks seemed to be out to get him.

"And rightly so. Imagine! Running your own company at such a young age."

Lillie almost choked. She pulled her hand away. "What?"

He looked puzzled. "Maybe I misunderstood."

"I doubt it. Gram tends to adopt any version of reality that makes her happy, whether it bears close resemblance to the truth or not."

Seeing him start to scowl she quickly added, "She doesn't mean to lie. She just puts a spin on things. By the time she's told a story over and over, I doubt she has a clue what the real truth of the matter is. Actually, I worked for a large insurance company."

"I see."

Sensing a possible ally in her quest to help her grandmother, Lillie glanced at the glass cabinet behind the counter where they kept the desserts. "Look, Pastor Warner, I see we have scads of cherry pie left. How would you like a big piece of that, with ice cream, on the house?"

"I'd love it."

He smiled and Lillie's blush deepened. No wonder the church was running out of room. The Front Porch Christian congregation had to be overflowing with eligible women now that James was its pastor. That thought made her cringe. The last thing she wanted was to give the impression she was making a play for him, too.

Considering the lousy marriage record of the last two generations of her family, she figured she was better off getting a dog or a cat. Matter of fact, if her apartment building in Chicago hadn't had rules against pets, she'd have had a sweet little dog to keep her company long ago.

Leading the way between the tables, Lillie ducked behind the counter, washed her hands, then concentrated on dishing up the cherry pie, topping it with enough ice cream to nearly hide the crust.

"Whoa," James said, unzipping his jacket and settling himself on a stool. "That's plenty." When she put the dish in front of him he asked, "Aren't you going to join me?"

"Yes, but not to eat." Lillie leaned a hip against the opposite side of the counter and struck a nonchalant pose. "Gram made fried pies and insisted I eat a whole one this afternoon. That is seriously heavy food. I may never be hungry again."

James laughed. "Okay. But you look like a lady with something on your mind. Why don't you sit down and we'll talk while I eat?"

"I'll stand, thanks. But I would like to ask you about my grandmother."

"Sure. Just a sec." He bowed his head and murmured a blessing on his food.

Lillie felt more ill at ease than she had since puberty. How could she have forgotten the practice of saying grace? Darla Sue always used to insist upon it at mealtime when she was little, even though Grandpa Max refused to participate. She supposed, given their strained home life, Darla Sue had considered herself lucky that Max was there at all. What a sad existence.

Looking at James, Lillie was struck by the openness of his expression, the kindness in his dark eyes as he said, "Okay. Shoot. What's bothering you? I'll be glad to help if I can."

"Do you know about my grandfather?" Lillie asked.

"In what regard?" He forked a large bite of pie into his mouth and waited for her to answer.

Good. The man wasn't the kind to carry tales. That made Lillie more inclined to confide in him. "According to Gram, Max has run off with a floozy. Is that true?"

To James's credit he didn't strangle. He did, however, cough into his napkin. "I wouldn't put it quite that way. Since Miss Darla obviously told you about her problems, I won't be breaking a confidence if I answer. Yes, he did leave. And with a woman."

"A member of your congregation?"

"Unfortunately." His eyebrows arched and Lillie noticed that there was a little gray in them, the same as that peppering his dark hair at the temples.

"I take it she's another senior citizen?"

"Um, no. I think Gloria's about forty, forty-five."

Lillie gasped. "Whew!"

"My sentiments exactly," James said. "It's a touchy situation."

"I suppose I should ask if you know if Max is okay but I can't say he and I bonded the way Gram and I did. He never liked me much and he didn't bother to hide his feelings."

"That's too bad," James said.

"Yes, it is. No matter how hard I tried I

don't think I ever managed to please him." She decided to change the subject rather than dwell on past unpleasantness. "So, how's the pie?"

"Great. Did you bake it?"

Lillie gave a nervous laugh. "Me? Not hardly. You've seen the full extent of my talent in the kitchen. I can scoop ice cream and cut pie. Period."

"You're not a practicing Southern Christian like your grandmother?"

The question was delivered so deadpan Lillie almost missed the inside joke. The twinkle in his eye gave him away and she chuckled. "Oh, I get it. You mean, because of all the social eating they do. I used to go to church with Gram when I was younger but I haven't attended services in a long time. Guess none of the dinner-on-the-ground genes were passed on to me. I don't even own a casserole dish or a Crock-Pot."

"You're a lost soul, aren't you?"

"Not literally, if that's what you're fishing for. I went forward at a revival when I was thirteen." She decided not to expound on her lack of recent churchgoing.

"Glad to hear it." James continued to enjoy his pie. "So, what can I do for you? Is your grandmother grieving? I haven't been able to convince her to talk to me since Max left. I've stopped by several times in the past few weeks but she won't even let me in the house."

"Actually, she seems more upbeat than she has for years. What I'm worried about is her mind. I think she's out of touch with reality."

"In what way?"

"Well, for starters, she's letting a bad hair day keep her from coming to work and that's not at all like her."

"I see. Will you be staying long? If so, you might want to take her to the doctor for a checkup. You know, make sure she's mentally and physically sound."

Lillie nodded. "I'd thought of that. Actually, I was planning to move back to Gumption for good."

His head snapped up and his eyes seemed to brighten.

"Wonderful! Darla Sue will be thrilled. What did she say when you told her?"

"I haven't told her. Not yet." Lillie made a dour face in spite of the smile the preacher was beaming at her. "I quit my job when I left Chicago. Gram isn't going to like hearing that. She's always had a really strong work ethic."

"Except lately," James observed with a nod toward the kitchen. "I know she's playing hooky. That was one of the reasons I stopped by this evening. I'd heard you were back in town and I thought…"

"You didn't come here to eat? You took free pie under false pretenses? What kind of preacher are you?"

"Oh, I'm a hungry one," he answered with a grin. "But I could have grabbed a quick meal at the sandwich shop. I came here to see if I could find out how Darla Sue was really doing. I was afraid she might be putting on a brave front for my benefit."

"I don't think so. Except for her hair, she seemed fine when I showed up on her doorstep this afternoon."

"Then we can probably stop worrying about her and concentrate on praying for your grandfather."

Lillie made another face. "You can pray for Max if you want to but not me. And while you're at it, you might as well say a few words for my father. Turns out he was just as big a skunk as my granddad is."

Chapter Three

James wondered what he should have said to Lillie after her telling outburst. There were few instances since his ordination when he'd felt so unable to offer words of wisdom. Then again, he hadn't been a member of the clergy for nearly as long as his age would indicate.

Walking down Third Street toward the church parking lot where he'd left his motorcycle, he studied the old buildings on the square. Glow from the streetlights muted their flaws and made them seem sturdier, but they were still clearly antiquated.

Sadly, that was true of his church, too. Gumption Front Porch Christian was so small it was a wonder the congregation hadn't sold that sanctuary and moved on long ago. Yes, it had its namesake front porch and a quaintly charming stone facade but it lacked many necessary elements, not the least of which was adequate on-site parking.

Inside, wooden pews that bore the patina of age barely provided enough room for the regulars to squeeze in. Add a few visitors and they had to pull folding chairs out of the Sunday-school rooms and place them in the aisle to accommodate everyone.

Not only was that solution awkward, it was unsafe. If folks got up before the end of the service, there was a good chance they'd trip and fall before they reached the exits. Heaven forbid, literally, they ever had an emergency that required quick evacuation. Something had to be done, and soon.

He gave a tuneless whistle. Sudden rustling in a nearby tree led his gaze upward even though it was almost too dark to see. By approaching the tree trunk and leaning left, he was able to peer through the clusters of tiny white blossoms and catch a glimpse of what had drawn his attention. Two bright eyes reflected the dim light enough for him to tell that the creature definitely wasn't a squirrel. Judging by the pansylike face and pitiful mewing, it was a kitten. A very young kitten.

James wasn't particularly fond of cats. As far as he was concerned their place was in a barn, catching mice, not underfoot in a house. It was, however, one of God's creatures. And he was a servant of the Lord. Therefore, he assumed it was his duty to either affect a rescue or find someone who would.

Craning his neck to watch the kitten, he tried to recall how long it had been since he'd shinnied up a tree. Twenty years? Probably. Except for his motorcycle riding he'd never been as athletic as most boys. While they'd been out playing baseball and football, he'd been doing his homework or reading his dad's copy of the *Wall Street Journal*.

That had prepared him for his initially successful foray into the business world but it hadn't satisfied his soul or equipped him to deal with the perfidy of his partners or the infidelity of his late wife, which was why he'd eventually chucked his old life and escaped to the Ozarks.

He smiled. He could identify with Lillie Delaney's decision to quit her job and head for the hills. Although Gumption hadn't been his point of origin, it had served the same purpose. He, too, had come here to the South to start over. Perhaps he should have told her so. Then again, it was his job to listen and offer wise counsel, not spout off about his own life history the first chance he got.

Approaching the base of the tree, he reached up as far as he could. The frightened kitten hissed and backed away, trembling so badly that some of the tiny flower petals around it shook loose and drifted down.

"Come on, cat," he cajoled, wiggling his fingers. "Don't you know a friend when you see one?"

Obviously, the answer was no.

James withdrew, planning his next move as he brushed the shed blossoms off his jacket. He looked around. Few good citizens of Gumption were on the street at this time of night and those who were were judiciously avoiding eye contact. Either they knew there was a cat stuck in the tree or they still considered him an outsider, even after nearly a year. Either was possible. Both were likely.

If he were a hungry, scared animal, what would bring him to his rescuer? *Food.* He needed a big handful of something cats found irresistible.

It was quicker and easier to backtrack to DD's than to fire up his bike, ride home and raid his refrigerator.

Lillie had locked the front door when she'd let him out of the café so he circled around back. That door, too, was locked, but at least there was a porch light to see by.

Unwilling to give up so easily, James took off his jacket and rolled up his shirtsleeves, then cautiously lifted the top of the battered green Dumpster that sat against the brick wall. The fumes that instantly filled his nostrils were so strong, so disgusting, he dropped the lid with a bang.

Gasping, he turned away, grabbed a deep breath, held it and tried again. Judging by the smell, there were fish scraps in this garbage bin old enough to vote!

He was gingerly lifting aside a crumpled cardboard box when someone directly behind him said, "I don't believe it," and startled him so much he lost his hold on the lid once again. It thwacked him on the forearm before he could jump clear.

He whirled, uttering a heartfelt "Ow!" There stood Lillie Delaney, arms folded across her chest, giving him a look that intimated she'd caught him in the middle of a robbery. Then the corners of her mouth started to twitch and lift.

"Hello, again," she said, half laughing. "If you were *that* hungry, why didn't you ask for a second piece of pie?"

"I'm not doing this for myself," James explained. "It's for the cat."

She scanned the compacted gravel at his feet, then bent to peer behind the Dumpster. "What cat?"

"The one in the tree by the church." He couldn't help grinning back at her in spite of the pain in his forearm. "It's a long story." He started to rub his smarting arm, then realized how dirty he'd gotten and stopped. "Could you spare a paper towel? I'd like to clean up."

She stepped out of the doorway and held the screen for him. "Go on in and use the restroom. I'll wait for you."

"Thanks."

He made short work of scrubbing himself clean, rejoined her, and watched her secure the back door with a key as he put his jacket back on.

"I was looking for some tasty tidbit to use to lure a kitten out of a tree," he explained. "I was going to ask you for some scraps but the door was locked and I figured…"

"You figured a little Dumpster diving was called for. I see. And what were you going to do if your cat wouldn't come down for a treat?"

"Hey, it's not my cat."

"Finders keepers," Lillie taunted.

James fell into step beside her as she started down the sidewalk. "I didn't exactly find it," he argued. "It found me. It's not my fault God gave Adam dominion over all the animals."

"You think that command rubbed off on you?"

"Sure, why not? I just don't know much about cats."

Lillie laughed. "Well, you won't often see their skeletons in trees. Come on. Show me this kitty you can't handle. Gram has owned more cats than I can count over the years. I've always had a way with them."

* * *

Lillie understood the problem before she even saw the kitten. It had instinctively clambered up the tree and was now too frightened to descend. Yes, it would probably eventually get hungry enough to come down on its own but temperatures were still dropping into the forties or lower every night and she hated to let it suffer needlessly.

Therefore, either she or the preacher was going to have to leave the ground in order to stage a rescue. She sincerely hoped it was going to be him.

They stood together beneath the tree and studied the situation. To Lillie's dismay the trunk was barely six inches in diameter. Worse, it was a Bradford pear, an ornamental tree noted for its brittle nature.

She made a face. "Rats."

"No, I think it's a cat," James quipped.

She gave him a cynical look. "We'll need a ladder."

"Why? If you can't get him to come down I could just give you a little boost and... No?"

"No. Neither of us should climb that tree. Those branches won't support us." She saw him glance at her figure, then quickly look away without comment. If he thought she was too hefty, he was good at hiding his opinion.

"I mean," Lillie said, "this kind of tree is pretty, especially when it blooms in the spring, like now, but it's also notorious for breakage. I wouldn't dream of trusting it to hold either of us."

"Oh."

"So, do you have a ladder?"

"I think there's one in the church basement. Wait here. I'll go see."

"Bring a flashlight, too," she called after him.

"Right."

Watching him jog away toward the old rock church, she was taken by how well he moved—for an older guy. He must be, what, forty? Maybe forty-five, she concluded, which made him about ten years older than she was. Not that it mattered. It wasn't James Warner's mature good looks or even his calling that had impressed her. It was his caring heart. Most of the men she knew would have walked right on by the poor kitten and never even considered rescuing it.

Making good use of her time while she waited for the ladder, Lillie began to speak to the animal softly, coaxingly, calmly. The kitten's squeaky pleas mellowed. Soon it was answering her voice with a mew that seemed to imply trust and affinity.

Lillie stood close to the tree trunk. It was girdled by several rings of even holes, evidence that a woodpecker had been visiting to clear it of accessible insects.

She extended her arm slowly, deliberately, and rested her hand in the joint of the lowest limb as she continued a high-pitched murmur. "Good kitty. That's a sweet baby."

Whiskers tickled her fingertips. One quick grab that missed and she'd undo the trust she'd established. Forcing herself to be patient, she waited till she felt the kitten rub against her hand, then gently curled her fingers around its tiny body and lifted it down.

"What a good baby," she cooed, holding and cuddling it. "Your uncle James is going to be so proud of you."

Speaking of which… She squinted toward the church. Some of the lights in the rear were on so she knew he was inside. Surely he should have located the ladder and hauled it out by now. What could be keeping him?

James stood amid the carnage and stared. Whoever had ransacked the church basement and smashed the nativity figures had done so deliberately. There was no way the damage had been accidental. It was too widespread.

A shadow darkened the doorway at the top of the stairs. He tensed. "Who is it?"

"Me," Lillie said. "What are you doing down there—building a ladder from scratch?"

"No." He heard the steps creak. "Stop! Don't come down here. I'm coming up."

"Okay. You don't have to yell at me."

He quickly joined her. "Sorry. I didn't mean to raise my voice. I was just upset. You won't believe what I found."

She had continued to cuddle the gray-and-white striped kitten. Now, she smiled and held it up as he joined her at the top of the stairs. "You won't believe what I found, either. Look. It came to me."

"Terrific." He brushed past her and headed down the hall.

Lillie followed. "Well, you might act a little pleased. At least we won't have to risk life and limb to rescue it."

"Yeah, well, I have other things on my mind right now. Somebody has been fooling with the storage in the basement and made a real mess."

"You're kidding."

"No. I'm calling the cops."

"Wait. I saw a big motorcycle parked out back. Maybe whoever broke into the church rode that and we should disable it so they can't get away."

"Not everybody who rides a bike is dangerous. The Harley's mine." He sensed that she'd stopped behind him in the hallway so he ordered, "Stay with me. Like you said, we're not sure the vandals are gone. I wouldn't want you getting hurt."

"Or Fang, either."

"Fang?" James knew he was scowling at her and the kitten but he allowed himself the momentary expression of disdain. "You named *that* Fang?"

Lillie giggled. "Sure. Why not?" She sobered. "Sorry. I know you're in no mood for jokes. And I apologize for overreacting about the motorcycle. Go ahead and make your call. We'll be right behind you."

James paused and let his gaze travel over her. "Try not to move around too much or we'll have to vacuum this place. Your hair and clothes are full of those little white flower petals and you're shedding them all over everything."

The local sheriff had lived in that area his whole life. Therefore, he and Lillie were well acquainted. She was sitting outside on the concrete steps to the sanctuary, the kitten napping cozily inside the front of her pink nylon jacket, when he arrived.

She wasn't surprised to see him but she was a little taken aback that there was now so much of him. Caleb Frost was *twice* the man he used to be and a goodly portion of him lapped over his belt in a jiggling roll.

She smiled. "Hey, Caleb."

"Well, well, little Miss Lillie. I heard you was back. Finally got your fill of Chicago, eh?"

"Something like that." She got to her feet so she could speak more quietly, more privately, taking care to secure the kitten as she moved. "Tell me, Caleb. What's going on around here? We never used to have trouble like this in Gumption."

"Times change," the lawman said. He eyed the church. "You meet the new preacher?"

"Yes. He seems okay. Why?"

"Nothin'. Just seems a tad odd that nobody had any problems with this church, or any other, till he showed up."

"He must have come with credentials and good recommendations. The pastoral search committee would never have hired him otherwise."

"That's true I guess." He snorted. "'Course, I don't belong to this particular church so I can't say for certain."

"It's not the name over the door that matters and you know it, Caleb."

He guffawed. Lillie wouldn't have been surprised to see him slap his knee, too.

"You have growed up, haven't you, missy? Well, just you remember, folks around here take care of their own. Been doin' it for more years than you've been on this earth."

"Like Annabelle Pike, you mean?" Lillie

straightened and stood tall with the remembrance of her local historical idol. It had been a long time since she'd thought of Annabelle's bravery back in 1838 and the memory strengthened her. If that pioneer woman could face down the whole U.S. Army to save the life of a Cherokee baby she'd rescued from the Trail of Tears, Lillie could certainly stand up to the likes of Caleb Frost.

The portly sheriff chose to disregard her antagonistic attitude. "I hear the preacher's got another problem. Best be gettin' inside to see about it before he gripes to the city council." He touched the brim of his cap and gave as much of a bow as his pendulous gut would permit. "Evening, Miss Lillie."

She waited until he'd turned his back and entered the church before she gave in to the childish urge to make a face and stick out her tongue at him.

James was sitting behind his desk when Lillie entered the office a half hour later. "I just saw Caleb leave," she said. "What did he say?"

"Same thing he said when the church and

my Harley were egged a few weeks ago. He's sure I did something to tick somebody off." James raked his fingers through his hair. "I wish I knew if he was right."

"Even if he is, it's not your fault. I'm sure that whatever you said or did, you had the right motives."

"Thanks."

"I understand this congregation has grown a lot since you became its pastor."

"It has. And we really do need bigger facilities, which is why we're in the process of working up plans for a whole new building. I suspect my problems may be because of that."

"There are always folks who resist change, but if this church is really too small, it's your duty to enlarge it, right?"

"That was my conclusion."

"Then you have nothing to blame yourself for. You can't please everybody." She smiled. "And certainly not in a small town like Gumption. Like they say, stub your toe once around here and a dozen people fall down."

James had to smile. "Yeah?"

"Yeah. Gram used to tell me that if I sneezed, a hundred folks would say, 'God bless you,' before the dust had settled. That used to strike me as a drawback but now I sort of see it as a comfort."

"It should be."

Still carrying the kitten, this time on the outside of her jacket, she slowly strolled around the room. "You've cleaned up this office nicely. I used to come to youth group here on Saturdays and I remember all the stacks of books and paper Brother Smallwood had piled everywhere. It was a real mess."

"I moved a lot of that stuff to the basement but I kept it for the day when the church has its own library. That's just one more reason why we need a larger building."

"I suppose it will be expensive."

"God will provide."

James wasn't about to admit that the idea of borrowing all that money for the building project occasionally gave him pause, in spite of the hours of prayer and discussion he and his deacons and trustees had dedicated to the decision. He really did believe God was in control. Looking back, the handiwork of the Lord was easy to see. Looking forward, however, it was a little more difficult to be positive you were on the right track.

He huffed. Who was he kidding? It was a *lot* more difficult.

Lillie paused and zeroed in on a framed diploma hanging on the far wall. "Wow. Massachusetts? I'm impressed. You actually graduated from a seminary there?"

"Yes." James joined her, his hands stuffed nonchalantly into the pockets of his jeans. "I wasn't raised in the church like a lot of people are. When I finally gave my life to the Lord I wanted to do it right, so I decided to go to school to learn about the Bible. One thing led to another and here I am."

"Amazing." Lillie read aloud from the certificate. "James Robert Warner."

"That's me." To his consternation, she began to giggle. "What's so funny?"

"You really don't know?" Chuckling, Lillie turned to face him. A wide grin split her face and made her blue eyes sparkle with delight.

"Know *what?*" Of all the reactions he'd had to his higher education, hers was the strangest. He couldn't imagine that she disapproved, yet she certainly wasn't taking his hard-won ordination seriously.

"You've missed a great opportunity here,"

she said, obviously struggling to keep from breaking up as she spoke.

"I have?"

"Yes. You shouldn't go by Brother James or Brother Warner."

"I shouldn't?"

"No." A chortle shook her shoulders and roused the kitten, so she absently scratched it behind the ears. "This may not be Georgia or Louisiana but it's still the South," she said. "If you really want to fit in around here you *have* to start calling yourself Brother Jim Bob!"

His eyebrow arched. "That's a joke, right?"

"Yes. And no. In case you haven't noticed, most of us have two first names."

"Like Darla Sue?" He paused, smiling. "So, what's your other name?"

"Just Lillie."

"Oh, no, you don't. You started this. Come on. If you don't fess up I'll keep asking around until somebody tells me. What's your middle name, Miss Lillie?"

She pulled a face. "I forget."

He crossed his arms and shook his head. "Uh-uh. Not good enough. Shall I guess? Sue? Lynn? Mary?"

"Much worse than that," she said with resignation. "My mother was a flower lover. She couldn't decide which of four names to use so she tagged me with all of them. I'm officially Lillie Rose Iris Daisy Delaney."

Grinning, James was incredulous. "You have to be joking."

She snorted derisively. "I wish I was. You'd be doing me a big favor if you didn't use any of them. Okay?"

"Okay. As long as you don't start calling me Jim Bob and inspire everybody else to do it, too."

She stuck out her hand. "Deal."

As James took it to shake on their agreement, he was struck by how soft her skin was, how lovely she looked with those loose flower petals dusting her silky light brown hair.

He quickly pulled away. The last thing he intended to let himself do was admire another woman. He'd been married once and had experienced the agony of his wife's disloyalty and their subsequent divorce. When she had died unexpectedly, he had still grieved, yet his mind was made up. Never again would he trust like that, love like that. It had hurt too much.

Besides, he reminded himself, he had work to do for the Lord. That was all he needed or wanted. His congregation was the only family he required and his life was already complete. Period.

Looking at Lillie and seeing her guileless smile, he wondered why, for the first time in years, he was tempted to question that sensible conclusion.

Chapter Four

Lillie had ended up taking Fang home to Darla Sue's with her because James had refused to consider himself permanently responsible for the kitten. She desperately needed a confidante so she decided to phone Chancy Boyd, an old friend who ran an antique shop in nearby Serenity.

"Lillie! Is that really you? It's great to hear from you after all this time," Chancy said. "Where are you staying? Are you moving back or just visiting?"

Lillie laughed. "It's good to hear your voice, too, Chancy. I'm here for keeps. I'll be staying with Gram for the time being. Her number's in the book but if you can't reach me there, feel free to call the café or stop in some time and we'll visit. Looks like I'm going to be spending a lot of time there, at least for a while."

"I can't believe it's really you. Wait till I tell Nate."

"Who's Nate?"

Chancy giggled. "My gorgeous new husband. I'm Chancy Collins now."

"Congratulations!" Lille was happy for her friend but a bit envious, too. "I'm never getting married. You won't believe what's happened here. Grandpa ran off with another woman. A younger one. Gram is fit to be tied and I don't blame her."

"Wow, you really stepped into a mess, didn't you?"

"That's not the half of it," Lillie said with a shake of her head. "I haven't told Gram I'm here for keeps and I've already gotten stuck with an extra cat—a kitten to be exact. I hope she's not going to mind my bringing it home with me. If I'm cautious, maybe she won't notice."

That made her friend giggle. "Oh, dear. How senile is she? I mean, wouldn't most people notice?"

"Not as easily when they already have a

houseful of cats," Lillie explained. "At least I hope not. I'm standing here in the kitchen, talking to you, and there's a calico on the chair, an orange tabby rubbing against my leg and three more gray-and-white ones sleeping in the corner by their food dishes."

"You need a dog," Chancy teased. "Nate's grandparents have a wonderful one."

"Well, right now I seem to be the proud owner of a really cute kitten and that's enough, thanks." She sighed. "It truly is good to hear your voice. I've missed living close enough to get together with you when I need a pal."

"Call anytime. Honest. Or stop by the shop when you get over this way. It's not far. Nate's building us a house on the Collins farm but until it's done we're still living in the apartment over the shop, so I'm always here."

"It's a deal. Well, I'd better go. The kitten is getting restless and I'm not sure where Gram is. I want to introduce him to the older cats before she has a chance to tell me they won't get along."

"Will they?"

"I think so. All of Gram's cats have been

altered so there shouldn't be any territorial squabbles. I'm hoping one of the old mama cats will adopt this baby and protect it. I'll keep you posted. And look for me soon. I'll do my best to get over your way so we can really visit."

"Sounds wonderful. Take care."

"You, too. Bye."

Putting her cell phone into her pocket, Lillie placed the kitten on the floor and watched. The other cats accepted the baby with curiosity, yet few hisses or arched backs. Lillie relaxed. If her grandmother took to the new resident as well as her house cats had, all would be well.

Trying to slip the orphan cat into Darla's horde without question didn't bother Lillie nearly as much as the fact that her grandmother had continued to treat her as if she'd never been away.

Lillie decided it was time for a serious discussion. She found her grandmother in the living room, sat down beside her on the sofa and brought up the subject of her permanent relocation.

"I've decided to move back to Gumption," she announced, taking Darla Sue's hand so she couldn't use the TV remote and create too much of a distraction.

The older woman blinked and then smiled. "'Bout time. What took you so long?"

"I thought I was happy in the city."

"Bah! You might of fooled yourself but you didn't fool me. You never did belong in Chicago." She poked a finger under the elastic edging of the shower cap to scratch her scalp. "All a body needs is right here. I've always known that."

"Then why didn't you try to stop me from leaving?"

"I couldn't make a choice like that for you. If you hadn't left, you might have spent your whole life wonderin' if you'd missed something. Now you know you didn't. And you'll be more content right here."

"I guess that's true," Lillie agreed. "I'll need to find a new job and a place to live, though." She was taken aback when Darla Sue's head snapped up, her eyes growing suspiciously moist.

"You've already got both, girl."

Lillie shook her head soberly. "I know you'd let me stay with you as long as I wanted and work at the café for a while but that's not fair to you."

"What's not fair?" Her lower lip had begun to tremble though she'd lifted her chin defiantly. "If I wasn't tickled pink to have you here I'd say so. And as for the restaurant, it can use some younger blood." The slump of her shoulders made her look every one of her seventy-plus years. "I'm tired, honey. Wrung out. It's not just your grandpa's she-nanigans that's done it, either. I've worked hard all my life and I need a little break. I thought, with you back home, I'd be able to rest a tad."

"You can. I didn't mean I wouldn't help you out. I just thought…"

"Thought what? That I'd want my café to pass to anybody but you?"

"Well, you could always sell it and retire on the profits you earned."

"Now why would I do that?"

"So you could take it easy?" Lillie's brow furrowed. "I get the feeling I'm missing some-thing here. What is it you'd like to see happen?"

"Really and truly?"

"Yes."

The older woman sighed, nodded and patted the back of her granddaughter's hand. "You may be sorry you asked."

"I'll take my chances. Shoot."

"Well, first off, I'd like you to move in here with me, at least till your life settles down. That way you won't have to worry about paying rent and I'll have some pleasant company. Somebody to talk to that says more than *meow*. The cats are fine company but they can't carry on much of a conversation, if you know what I mean."

"Okay. So far, so good. Go on."

"And I'd like for you to work at the café with me, learn the ropes, so you can take over if I want to do something else once in a while. If I was to get sick and couldn't work, the place would really suffer."

"It's suffering now," Lillie told her. "Helen and Rosie are trying but they're not keeping up very well."

"I was hopin' they'd step in and do what needed to be done if I wasn't there but now I see that the good Lord had other plans. His way is fine with me."

"Meaning you want me to manage the place? Okay. I'm good with numbers and I know I can learn how to order supplies if you explain the process to me. Anything else?"

Darla Sue began to grin like one of her pet cats caught with fresh feathers on its chin. "Yup. I'd like to see you find a nice local boy, settle down, get married and give me a passel of great grandbabies."

Lillie jerked her hand away. "Whoa! Where did *that* come from?"

"You asked."

"Yes, but I thought we were talking about you, not me."

"Told ya you wouldn't like it."

"It's not that, Gram. It's just that I've decided I'm not the marrying kind."

"Who says?"

"I do. I'm too independent. Too stubborn." *Too old and set in my ways.* "And you have to admit I'm a little short of good male role models."

"At least you know what *not* to look for."

Shaking her head, Lillie stared off across the cozy living room, seeing glimpses of the past instead of the flowered wallpaper and chintz curtains. "Look what happened to Mom, to you. I thought Dad was a wonderful man. And Grandpa Max might have been sort of grumpy but I never dreamed he'd just take off the way he did. I'm a *terrible* judge of men!"

Darla cackled. "You're probably as good at it as any woman. None of us can predict what the future will bring. All we can do is hang in there and try to pay attention when the good Lord is workin' in our lives." She smiled sweetly. "Do you think you made up your mind to come home, just when I needed you most, without a little special prodding from heaven?"

"Of course, I did." Lillie made a face. "Well, maybe not entirely. But I'd been thinking about doing it for a long time."

"And then, one day, you got serious?"

"Something like that, yes."

"Think what you like." She grinned. "Just remember, 'the Lord works in mysterious ways, His wonders to perform.'"

Lillie considered the opening tailor-made. "Speaking of spiritual things, why have you been playing hooky from church? It's not all because of your hair, so don't bother using that excuse."

"Who said I was goin' to? I just decided not to go, that's all."

"Brother James has been wondering about you. He's concerned."

"Is he, now? And how do you know that?"

"I met him. He came into the café to ask about you and we got to talking."

"Oh?" Gray eyebrows arched quizzically. "Do tell."

"There's nothing much to tell," Lillie insisted. "He ate a piece of pie and left."

"That's all?"

"Well…almost. I heard a noise out back by the Dumpster and found him looking for scraps to coax a kitten out of a tree so I helped him do it."

"Ah, so that's where it came from."

Uh-oh. "Where what came from?"

"The extra mouth to feed." Darla Sue pointed across the room to where several of her cats had gathered, including Fang. "I may be getting old but I can still tell a full grown cat from a kitten."

"He's really cute. Is adding one more so bad?"

"Not to me it isn't, but my neighbors are already het up about the ones I've got so I had to promise not to adopt any more. 'Fraid you'll have to take that cat back to the preacher."

"Oh, dear. I told him you wouldn't mind keeping it."

"Sorry. Guess you'll just have to tell him I do mind."

"He has a lot on his plate right now. It would help soften the blow if I could also tell him to expect you back in church this coming Sunday."

"You blackmailing me, girl?"

"I certainly hope so," Lillie answered with a widening grin. "How about it?"

"You goin' with me?"

She shrugged. "I suppose I could."

"Then I'll go," Darla Sue said, "but first I'm gonna get this hair cut off so I look halfway decent."

"Wonderful! I'll make you an appointment at the beauty shop."

"Naw. No need to go to all that trouble. I'll grab scissors and be done with it in two shakes."

Undeterred, Lillie reached for the telephone. There were some things she wasn't willing to give up for the sake of economy. Her grandmother was already hiding from her friends due to bad hair color and she wasn't about to let the eccentric older woman add a shaggy, homemade haircut to her list of lame excuses to act like a hermit.

As they approached the church the following Sunday morning, Lillie was thankful that she'd been able to talk her grandmother out of cutting her own hair. The way it had been professionally styled, with soft feathering against her forehead and cheeks, it made her look years younger in spite of its natural gray color. Lillie had also bought her a modest, curly gray wig in case she decided at the last minute that her new hairdo was too modern-looking.

The one thing Lillie hadn't done was return Fang to the church. After trying to catch James in his office three times and failing, she'd given up, planning to broach the subject after Sunday services. In the meantime, she'd kept the kitten in her bedroom and had, unfortunately, bonded with it far more than she'd wanted to.

Darla Sue was greeted warmly and complimented on her new look by nearly everyone she encountered as she and Lillie entered the church.

"See? I told you your hair looked wonderful like that."

The older woman huffed. "Ha. I feel like I've been scalped. I'll go down to the Senior Center later in the week and give Wanda another call on that picture phone, then we'll see about it."

She elbowed Lillie in the ribs and nodded toward the place where James had been greeting parishioners. He'd glanced up, spotted them and begun grinning from ear to ear. "Well, well. Looks like our preacher's mighty glad to see you."

"I'm sure it's you he's glad to see," Lillie insisted, returning his smile.

"Maybe. 'Course, I don't recall that he ever paid that much attention to me before you came back to Gumption." She held up one thin hand to whisper behind it. "He cleans up pretty good, don't he? Looks like a different fella when he takes off that leather jacket and dresses proper."

Lillie agreed that James did look nice in his dark suit and tie, although she found she missed the casual quality of his motorcycle jacket and jeans. He currently fulfilled his congregation's idea of the way a minister should dress but the way he'd looked when she'd first met him had made him seem far more approachable. More individual. More unique.

Together, Lillie and her grandmother joined James at the door to the sanctuary. Lillie was relieved when he immediately reached for Darla Sue's hand instead of hers.

"I'm so glad to see you, Mrs. Howell. It's a pleasure to have you back with us."

"Wouldn't be here if it wasn't for her," Darla Sue grumbled, nodding at Lillie. "She made me come."

His eyes twinkled as they met Lillie's. "Then I owe you my thanks."

Before Lillie could respond, Darla Sue said, "If you hadn't taken that cat back I'd be home in my garden where I belong, tending the flowers as usual."

"I beg your pardon?"

"That kitten you found. When I told Lillie I couldn't keep it she made me promise to come to church to make it up to you for returning it."

"Oh?" One of his eyebrows arched as he shifted his attention to Lillie. "I think I'm missing something here. What did you do with the poor little thing?"

She blushed. "Well, I didn't hurt it or

abandon it, if that's what you're thinking. I stopped by your office more than once to try to arrange to bring you Fang but I never could catch you in."

"And?"

Pressing her lips into a thin line and giving him the most disgusted look she could muster, she confessed, "And, I took him back home and kept him. He's spent the past week shut up in my bedroom at Gram's."

"I see."

"No, you don't," Lillie said flatly. "You found Fang and that makes you responsible for him, whether you like it or not. If we can't find him another home, you'll have to take him back."

"Really? Who says?"

"I do," Lillie insisted.

Beside her, Darla Sue piped up, "Me, too." Her jaw was set, her thin shoulders squared. "It's the Christian thing to do."

"I'm afraid precise instruction on adopting stray cats is not in the Scriptures," James said.

Lillie could tell he was fighting to keep a straight face because one corner of his mouth kept twitching with the beginnings of a lopsided smile.

Darla Sue wasn't going to be deterred. "Humph. Well, it should be. If you can't show a little charity, maybe I'm in the wrong church."

To Lillie's surprise and delight, James laughed. "Tell you what I'll do," he said, "I'll make a plea from the pulpit this morning and we'll try to find Fang a new home. How's that?"

"I s'pose it'll do," the elderly woman said. She grabbed her granddaughter's arm. "Come on, honey. Let's go find us a pew before all the good ones in the back are taken."

Lillie's expression was filled with mirth. Her laughing gaze caught James's and held it long enough to mouth "Sorry," before Darla Sue dragged her away.

As she glanced back at him, she noted that his eyes were bright and his shoulders were shaking with subdued amusement. He could have been upset, even angry, at being told what he had to do by a couple of cat-loving women who had no business interfering in his personal life, yet he'd chosen to treat the whole incident with humor. That spoke well of him.

Following her grandmother down the center aisle, Lillie smiled at the strangers who were greeting her as she passed. She hadn't attended church regularly for far too many years. Perhaps it was time to renew the old habit, to start reestablishing herself in Gumption, beginning here.

Choosing a home church would be easy. This congregation and its pastor were perfect. She already felt as comfortable with them as she did with her grandmother.

In truth, she realized with a start, she hadn't felt totally at peace until this morning when she'd walked into that welcoming sanctuary. Perhaps she had *come home* in more ways than one.

James took his place behind the pulpit and peered into the congregation, scanning it as he always did before beginning his sermon. Many of the people looking back at him were already dear friends.

He smiled slightly, admitting that the congregation also had its share of lemons and praying that he'd eventually be able to reach them, to sweeten their sour attitudes. Why couldn't they see what a precious gift from

God every moment of their life was? Why wasn't he able to wake them up to their true potential? That was his job, wasn't it?

Yes, but he couldn't *make* them see the truth any more than he could force them to believe in Jesus Christ the same way he did. It all boiled down to personal choice. Free will. Only God had the power to reach the lost. He was merely the Lord's messenger, doing the best he possibly could and praying constantly for wisdom and patience.

He finally spotted Lillie and her grandmother in the third row from the back, near the center aisle, and his joy increased. What a pair they made! It was no wonder Lillie was so self-assured and spunky, since she was related to a woman like Darla Sue Howell. He could have throttled Max when he'd heard of his escapades. It would be so much easier to pastor a flock if his wayward sheep didn't keep jumping the fences.

Visualizing that picture made James smile as the choir filed in and sat in the rows of chairs behind him. As soon as they were in place he said, "Good morning." He looked out over the congregation. "This morning, before we begin our service, I have a favor to ask of you all. It seems there is a kitten in need of a new home as soon as possible, and I've been appointed to find it that home."

Titters and the hum of soft-spoken comments made him broaden his smile. "Yes, I know. It's technically not my job. But we all need to try to do what's right even if it is an unusual request. If any of you know of a good home for the kitten, you can see me after church or talk to Mrs. Howell." He gestured. "She's sitting there in the back. And I'd also like to welcome her grand-daughter, Lillie Delaney. We're glad to have you here, Lillie."

In the front pew, mere feet from the pulpit, James saw two of the Childress sisters lean closer to whisper to their mother. The third sat ramrod straight beside her father, Charles, who happened to be one of the church deacons. All three sisters were still single and their parents had made no bones about wanting James to choose one of them to be his future wife. Now, it looked as if the entire family was miffed at him over his friendly greeting of Lillie.

Well, it couldn't be helped. He'd been married before and once was plenty. Before her death, his former wife had not only cheated on him with one of his nefarious business partners, they'd ended up betraying him financially, too. Of all the disappointments he'd had to face, his wife's blatant disloyalty had been the hardest to take.

As he'd often reiterated, he now viewed his church and his congregation as his family. He was their father, their brother, their confidant and in some cases he knew he was thought of as their son, particularly by some of the doting older women. As long as no one tried to pair him up and marry him off, that was just fine with him.

Chapter Five

As far as Lillie was concerned, church was a time for worshipping the Lord, not gossiping. Unfortunately, the folks in the pew directly behind her didn't seem to feel the same. She'd already overheard a lot more of their whispered conversation than she wanted to and it sounded as if they weren't going to stop chattering any time soon.

She was just about to turn around and shush them with as much diplomacy as she could muster when she heard her name mentioned.

"So *that's* Lillie Delaney," one woman hissed. "Didn't recognize her. I should of figured who she was, what with her sittin' by Darla Sue."

"Hush. They'll hear you."

You've got that right, Lillie thought.

"I don't care," came the answer. "She's got the nerve after what she did to my poor boy."

That made Lillie strain to hear more in spite of her misgivings. What could she possibly have done to the woman's son? She hadn't been back in town long enough to make enemies. At least she didn't think she had. Had he thought he'd gotten bad food or service at the café? It was all she could do to keep her head from swiveling to take a peek at whoever was speaking.

"He's never been the same," the woman said. "Ruined him for any other girl, that's what. I should have grandchildren by now. Would have, too, if it hadn't been for her."

Lillie was thunderstruck. What in the world could they be discussing? She hadn't dated anyone in Gumption since her teens and that was a long time for anyone to be holding a grudge. It was also too long for any normal man to carry a torch for her, assuming the speaker was right. As far as she knew, she hadn't broken any hearts or ruined anyone's life anywhere, especially not in that little town.

"Think the preacher's interested in her?" a male voice asked.

"Might be, I guess. He sure seemed happy she was here."

"Good," the man replied gruffly.

One of the women snapped back, "Good?"

"Yes, good. Far as I'm concerned, the more chances for him to get his comeuppance the better."

"Hush. I told you not to talk about that while we were here."

"I'll talk about it any time I please," he replied. "After what he and his friends did to me, I don't care what happens to him, as long as it's bad."

Lillie fidgeted in her seat. She could hear stirring behind her, as if the people who had been sitting there were getting up to leave. Surely they couldn't be. Not in the middle of the service. Still, she wanted to look to reassure herself that she would eventually be able to determine who had been speaking. She didn't intend to interfere in James's affairs but she figured it would be only sensible to warn him that someone in his congregation was angry with him.

When the collection plate was passed a few minutes later, she managed to glance over her shoulder without making her movements overt.

The pew behind her was empty.

Shaking James's hand at the door after the service, Lillie paused. "I need to speak with you."

"Of course." His brow knit. "Is the problem pressing?"

"I don't know," Lillie told him. "It's all very confusing. I wouldn't even mention it except..."

"Nonsense. Nothing is too trivial if it bothers you. When you've heard more of my sermons you'll know that's a favorite topic of mine. I keep telling people that no problem is too big or too small for God."

"In that case..." Others were pressing in behind her, anxious to shake the pastor's hand and be on their way.

"Tell you what," he said. "Why don't you and Mrs. Howell join me for dinner. I usually go over to the sandwich shop since DD's is closed on Sundays. We can talk things over while we eat."

"It's not Gram I want to talk about," Lillie said aside. "Maybe some other time." She started past him and was startled when he reached to stop her. He didn't actually touch her arm but his intent was obvious.

"Wait. I'm sorry. I misunderstood. I thought you wanted to discuss your family situation."

"Actually," Lillie replied, "it's *your* problems we need to talk about."

"My problems? I don't have any problems."

"Yes, you do, whether you're aware of them or not."

"In that case," James said, "why don't you wait around for a few minutes till the place clears out a bit more and we'll talk right here." He smiled at Darla Sue, who had been chatting with friends and had finally joined them. "You don't mind if Lillie doesn't go right home with you, do you, Mrs. Howell? I can drive her over to your house later."

The elderly woman's bright blue eyes sparkled. "Mind? No sirree. Not me. You two kids take your time. I'll go home and spruce up Fang. I was just talking to the Lassiter girl and I think she's going to adopt him." Her gaze settled on Lillie. "Don't look so forlorn. I made sure you'll have full visitation rights."

The silliness of that comment brought back Lillie's smile. "Thanks, Gram. I know it's for the best. I was already getting too attached to the little darling."

"Your mothering instinct kicked up, is all," Darla said. "Perfectly natural." She turned her attention to James. "She'll make a fine wife and mama."

He cleared his throat. "I'm sure she will."

Lillie wished the floor would open up and swallow her. Of all the things Gram could have said, why did it have to be a homespun declaration of her availability?

Well, she reasoned, there was no real harm done. When she and Brother James had their private chat, she'd simply assure him that she was *not* husband-hunting and everything would be fine.

From his reaction to Darla Sue's statement, she had to assume he was no more eager to find a mate than she was, although he was certainly attractive enough. Why he was single at his age puzzled her. Then again, he was probably wondering the same thing about her.

* * *

The church foyer had cleared out, leaving only Lillie, James and several of the ushers, who were straightening the chairs in some of the Sunday-school rooms and gathering up the unused bulletins.

"We shouldn't talk in my office if we can help it. Not unless somebody like my secretary. Mary June, is nearby and I think she's already left," James said. "Can't give anyone cause to gossip even though we aren't doing anything wrong."

"That's scriptural, isn't it?"

"Yes. Paul wrote in First Thessalonians, 'Abstain from all appearance of evil.'"

"Good advice," Lillie said. "Timeless."

"That can be said of the whole Bible."

She chuckled quietly. "Far be it from me to get into a discussion of scripture with a pro. How about walking me out to my car while we talk?"

"What car? Didn't you ride in with Darla Sue?"

"Oops. Sure did." She didn't try to subdue the silly grin that kept insisting it belonged on her face in spite of her desire to remain unruffled. "Okay, walk me to your car?"

He shrugged. "Sorry. I don't own one."

"Uh-oh." Lillie's eyes widened. "Am I going to be riding home on the back of your Harley?"

"Unless you want to be the one who drives it. I don't suggest that."

"I don't suppose you do."

"You have that deer-in-the-headlights look, Lillie. Would you like me to ask one of the ushers to wait and drive you home, instead?"

"No. I really do need to talk to you and if you think the motorcycle is safe transportation for both of us that's good enough for me." She led the way outside and started along the sidewalk that skirted the building's perimeter.

James followed. He had loosened his tie and the tight collar of his dress shirt and had stuffed his hands into his pockets so that he appeared a lot more laid-back. That made it much easier for Lillie to begin talking openly.

"I overheard some disturbing things in church this morning," she said.

He arched his eyebrows but remained silent.

"I wasn't eavesdropping on purpose. The people in the pew behind Gram and me were yakking like they were still out here in the parking lot. I couldn't help overhearing what they said."

"Okay. Go on."

"Gram is a bit hard of hearing so I don't think she heard the threats but I certainly did."

"Threats? What did they say?"

"Somebody doesn't like you."

He huffed quietly. "That's not a surprise. I can't preach the truth of the gospel without making enemies. It's always been like that, even back in Paul's time."

"I don't think this was about your preaching," Lillie said soberly. "The man said he hoped you got your comeuppance because of something you and your friends had done to him."

James stopped walking. "My friends?"

"Yes. It sounded to me as if he may have been dredging up the past. Is that possible?"

"I suppose it is."

She could tell by his expression and faraway look that he was reliving something unpleasant. "Why would anyone want to wish you unhappiness?" She refrained from adding that the speaker had tied that possible unhappiness to the pastor's supposed interest in her.

"I told you I came to the Lord late in life," James said. "Before I took this job I told the deacons and trustees all about my past."

"Was it very bad?"

"If you mean was I evil or criminal? No. But the same men who ruined me were responsible for taking other people's money under false pretenses, too."

"That's terrible. What happened?" She suspected she'd overstepped the bounds of propriety so she said, "Sorry, it's none of my business."

"I don't mind. As I said, it's not a deep dark secret. I got involved with a certain investment firm through my wife." He looked into Lillie's eyes and paused. "Yes, I was married. Once. Long ago. Elizabeth assured me that the men in question were longtime friends of her family and could be trusted, so I vouched for them. That was how small, unwary investors were sucked into their scheme and defrauded. By the time I figured out what was going on, there was nothing I could do to save the situation. Many innocent people went bankrupt as a result, including me."

"How awful."

"It was enlightening, that's for sure." He managed a wry smile. "When that firm was finally investigated and the truth came out, my business went down the tubes, too. My wife tried to blame everything on me."

"I'm so sorry."

"Don't be. Because of what happened I learned that my own intelligence and abilities were insufficient. Eventually that realization led me to turn to the Lord, so I can't fault the result. It was the process of getting there that hurt."

He'd started to walk again. Lillie kept pace. "I can only imagine. What happened to her? Your wife, I mean."

"She divorced me after I refused to take the fall for her and her friends. She was sentenced to probation while most of the others got jail time. Turns out she'd have been safer in prison. She was killed in a car wreck about a year later."

"Oh, dear. Do you think the man I heard talking could have been one of the old investors? Surely, you'd have recognized him if that was so, wouldn't you?"

"Not necessarily. I didn't know them all personally. I did see some of them in court while the trial was going on but I don't know that I'd remember their faces. My life had just fallen apart and I was pretty numb at the time."

"No wonder. How are you doing, now?"

"Better all the time," he said, his smile spreading as he gazed at her. "But you can understand why I prefer to remain single, can't you?"

"Absolutely. I was almost engaged when I lived in Chicago. The fact that we broke up before it was too late was a narrow escape. For both of us."

James laughed. "You may be right. Not everyone is cut out to be married."

"Sounds like the Apostle Paul, again."

"And James Robert Warner. The one thing I don't seem to be able to convince folks of is the seriousness of my decision to stay single. When I introduced you in the service this morning you'd have thought I'd committed an unpardonable sin."

"Why?"

Chuckling, he shook his head. "There were several eligible ladies sitting up front who looked daggers at me. And that was nothing compared to the cold stares I got from their parents! You have no idea what it's like to be considered an eligible bachelor."

"Hey, at least they don't call you an old maid behind your back."

"They do that to you? Preposterous."

"Yeah, well, maybe it isn't quite that bad but that's the gist of it. I don't know why people can't just leave us alone to live our lives the way we've chosen."

"They think they're doing us a favor," he said wisely. "And while we're talking about favors, thanks for letting me know what you overheard. I don't know how I can help the man who's so upset with me but perhaps I'll eventually get the chance to ask for his forgiveness."

Lillie paused and stared up at him. "Now there's where you and I differ. I'd want to figure out who he was so I could avoid him at all costs."

Climbing on board the Harley in her Sunday best was a trick Lillie wasn't sure she could accomplish. At least not grace-fully. She stood back, hands on her hips, and took stock of the situation.

James handed her a black helmet. "Here. Put this on."

"It's not my color," she quipped, taking it gingerly. "Besides, where's yours?"

"I only have one, so you get to wear it."

"I take it you don't usually carry passengers."

"Not as a rule, no." He began to smile. "The local gossipers should have a field day when they see us. First I mention you in church and now we're seen riding around town on my bike. I hope it won't bother you too much."

"Me? Naw. I'm used to ridiculous rumors. Remember, I grew up in Gumption."

"It must have been interesting, to say the least."

"If you're not from around here, I suppose it can be a bit off-putting. But these people mean well. They're really sweethearts, at least most of them are. They just tend to be a little clannish."

"A *little* clannish?" James laughed heartily.

"Okay, a lot," she replied, sharing his amusement.

He'd stepped back and was eyeing the motorcycle while clearly trying not to stare at Lillie. "Here's how we'll do this. I'll get on first."

"Fine with me," she said as she continued to smile. "I'm just glad I wore a full skirt this morning or I'd never be able to ride gracefully."

She ducked through the strap of her shoulder bag so it hung diagonally across her chest, then squared the helmet on her head while James watched. It fit better than she'd imagined it would.

"You need to fasten the strap for safety," he said.

Tilting up her chin, Lillie tried to do as he'd told her, failed, then presented herself to him for assistance. "Would you mind? I don't seem to have the hang of it."

"Sure."

Watching him through lowered lashes she suspected he was blushing, although with the healthy glow of his skin it was hard to tell. Thankfully, he had the helmet secured in seconds.

"There. Ready?" he asked.

"As ready as I'll ever be." She stood patiently while he started the motor, then held her skirt close and swung one leg over so she was seated behind him. The arrangement of her clothing preserved her modesty.

"You'd better hang on to me," James shouted over the roar of the engine as they pulled out of the parking lot.

Lillie knew he was merely being sensible but the idea of grasping him around the waist was a bit off-putting. It wasn't that she was afraid of him, it was simply that she didn't think it wise to be seen hugging him, even if it was for safety's sake. If she had given the situation more thought in the first place, she never would have put herself in such an awkward position, both literally and figuratively.

"Don't fight it!" James yelled.

"I beg your pardon?"

He turned his head slightly. "The corners. Lean into them with me. If you try to sit up too straight you're liable to throw off my balance and wreck us."

"Oh." Lillie tried to comply without revealing how badly she had misinterpreted his innocent statement. Too many years in the city had apparently left her quick to assume the worst. How long would it be, she wondered, before she was able to take folks at face value and not keep imagining ulterior motives where there were none?

"That's better," James called over his shoulder. "How do you like it?"

She had to admit she was enjoying the ride although she was careful to rationalize that it was the motorcycle that was making her heart race, not her proximity to its driver. "This is actually fun. I had no idea."

"Good." He paused, then added, "It's easier to balance if I go a little faster. Is that okay with you?"

"Sure!"

The word was hardly out of her mouth before he began to accelerate, leaving her no alternative but to wrap her arms securely around his waist.

She was grinning from ear to ear and hanging on for dear life as they roared past the sandwich shop. In the crowded parking lot, Lillie glimpsed at least three carloads of Front Porch Christian parishioners. Every person who looked up as they passed was staring, open-mouthed.

Lillie giggled. Local gossip was probably going to have them going steady by evening and half married before the end of the week!

He slowed as they approached Darla Sue's brick house and banked smoothly into the drive, coming to a stop behind her car.

Breathless, eyes bright, Lillie stepped off the bike. "Whew! When you give a person a ride, you don't kid around, do you?"

"I didn't scare you, did I?" James asked, clearly concerned. He dismounted and carefully balanced the Harley on its kickstand.

"No. Not at all." She was grinning as she unfastened the helmet, removed it and handed it to him. "But the gang at the sandwich shop sure got an eyeful as we passed. Did you see the looks on their faces when we raced by?"

"I didn't notice. Was it good?"

"Yes, and no. I have the feeling they'll have plenty to talk about this afternoon."

"Us, you mean?"

"Oh, yeah. But I don't mind if you don't. The way I see it, if Gram and the rest of them think you and I are involved, maybe they'll leave me alone and not keep trying to fix you up."

James smiled. "You know, that's not a bad idea. I wouldn't want to lie about it, of course, but I see no reason to explain otherwise if some people decide we're interested in each other. Do you?"

"Nope. The less said, the better. And knowing folks in Gumption, the less we're willing to talk about it, the more they're going to be sure we're an item."

He held out his hand. "In that case, consider me officially courting you, Miss Lillie. I can't think of anyone I'd rather pretend to be dating."

"Thanks. I think." She laughed lightly and grinned up at him as she shook his warm hand to seal the bargain.

It would be better, she decided quickly, if touching his hand wasn't quite so pleasing. Then again, that brief contact was nothing compared to the way she'd been forced by circumstances to hug him while riding home.

The excitement of the ride itself was what had made her heart race so, she concluded sensibly. That was all it was. A simple surge of adrenaline had created the exhilaration she had experienced—and was still feeling.

It couldn't be anything else.

It must not be because of her proximity to James.

She wouldn't let it be.

Chapter Six

Life at the restaurant finally resumed some normalcy thanks to Darla Sue's return to work, although it took several weeks of coming in even earlier than usual in order to whip the neglected kitchen back into shape, not to mention adequately restocking the larder and freezers.

Rosie had stayed on as cook's helper, much to Lillie's relief, and Helen was still waiting tables. On Helen's days off Lillie handled the front with part-time help from a teenager named Ruth Anne. The girl wasn't a practiced server but she made up for her lack of experience by being upbeat and enthusiastic.

It was nearly eight in the morning. Lillie

and her grandmother had already been working in the kitchen for several hours and were prepping vegetables while Rosie prefried bacon and made sausage gravy for the expected breakfast crowd.

"I had no idea how much work you had to put into keeping this place going," Lillie told Darla Sue. "No wonder you were away from home so much when I was younger."

"I didn't want to be. But it couldn't be helped. That's one reason why I asked you to work for me in your spare time and during summer vacations from school. I missed spending time with you."

"Even then you were planning for me to take over someday, weren't you?"

"It had crossed my mind a time or two." She busied herself tearing lettuce leaves into smaller pieces and filling rows of salad bowls while Lillie stood to one side and quartered fresh tomatoes.

"What amazes me is the way you remember how many of these dinner salads to make every day or what produce to order in the first place," Lillie said. "You keep all that information in your head?"

"Most of it," her grandmother answered.

"I suppose I should have written it down, like you've started doing, but I never seemed to lose track." She pulled a face. "Not until Max got me all befuddled, that is."

Lillie had purposely avoided earlier mention of her grandfather. She used this ready-made opportunity to ask, "Have you heard anything from him?"

"Nope. Nary a word. I suspect he's too busy with his girlfriend."

"I'm so sorry."

Darla Sue managed a smile. "Don't be sorry, honey. Max is Max. If the old fool aims to run off and make an idiot of himself over some floozy, there's nothing any of us can do about it."

"Did you know her? The floozy, I mean?"

Darla cackled softly. "Not well. She wasn't my kind of woman. All she cared about was her perfect hair and long, polished nails and wearing lots of gaudy jewelry." She snorted derisively and shook her head. "I'd like to have seen her do this job—or any decent job for that matter."

"You've been working too hard for a long time," Lillie said with affection. "I'm glad I can help you. I just don't know if I have enough drive or energy to give DD's the same kind of personal touch you always have."

"You'll do," Darla Sue said. "If I didn't think so, I'd close these doors today and never look back."

Lillie was encouraged. "Thank you. I promise I'll do my very best."

"Which reminds me," the older woman said, glancing at the clock on the wall over the soda machine, "It's almost time to open. You go ahead and unlock the door. I'll finish this myself."

"Okay."

Grabbing a ring of keys off a peg, she left the kitchen and headed for the glass front doors. Thankfully, business had picked up again. It looked as if there were enough people waiting outside this morning to fill nearly every chair and stool.

Lillie smiled and greeted them pleasantly. Rayford Evans was present, of course, and she recognized some of the usual couples from the senior housing complex down the road, too.

Her grin broadened with recognition. There, bringing up the rear and politely holding the door for the ladies to pass, was Brother James.

She caught his eye, waved briefly and hurried to pick up two coffeepots. If she'd learned anything in the weeks she'd been home it had been the importance of delivering fresh hot coffee to her customers first thing.

She started at the closest table and worked her way around the room, ending at the counter where James had made himself comfortable.

"Regular, not decaf, right?" she asked as she began to fill his cup.

He smiled. "Good memory. Do you also remember how I like my eggs?"

"Over hard, like rubber," she answered, grinning so broadly her cheeks hurt. "Chickens everywhere are complaining of the needless desecration."

Chuckling, he nodded. "If you say so." He eyed the kitchen. "How's your grandmother doing?"

"Better every day. Thanks for asking. And I think I'm beginning to get the hang of running this place, although it's a lot more work than it looks to be." She sobered and shook her head. "I can't believe how many little things disappear every day. Some folks even steal the salt shakers and those little hot-sauce bottles right off the tables."

"That is unbelievable. Maybe I need to preach a sermon on the evils of pilfering."

"It sure wouldn't hurt. I suppose they don't think it matters because the items are so small, but it hurts our business every time we have to replace something. It really can add up to a lot of expense in the long run."

"I'm sure it can."

"Speaking of crime, have you had any more vandalism problems at the church?"

"Not since the episode in the basement," James answered. "Have you heard anything else about who's mad at me?"

"Not a whisper." She jotted his order down as she said, "I'll go turn this in and see how Ruth Anne is managing with the other side of the room, then I'll be back and we can talk, okay?"

"Fine. I've already paid my morning calls at the county hospital over in Serenity. I have plenty of time."

"How is everybody doing?"

"All on the mend, praise the Lord."

"It must be hard to accept when things don't go well."

James nodded and took a sip of his coffee. "Yes, and no. It's like my motorcycle riding. Either the Lord is in charge of the lives of believers or He isn't. I may not like the results after I've prayed for a person's healing and they haven't gotten well, but I know I shouldn't argue with my Boss."

"I tend to argue with Him, anyway," she said, smiling, "which is probably why He has me slinging hash while you're in the pulpit. Be right back."

Darla Sue looked up from her place at the grill as Lillie delivered the orders she'd just taken. "I see your pastor friend is here again."

"The man has to eat," Lillie said.

"True. Thing is, he wasn't nearly as regular a customer till you came back to town."

"You were busy cooking. You probably just didn't notice."

"Horse feathers." She paused to expertly flip a row of hotcakes. "I may be getting a little forgetful but I know pretty much who all eats here and who doesn't. He want his eggs like rubber again?"

"Of course." Lillie couldn't help grinning. It seemed as if she was doing an inordinate amount of smiling lately, especially when James Warner was nearby. Well, it couldn't be helped. He was pleasant company, that was all. Good to talk to. Relaxing to be around. He had a quick mind and an equally wry sense of humor, making him the best company she'd kept in ages, man or woman.

"Order up," Rosie called.

Lillie balanced two platters on one arm, took the third in her free hand and headed back for the dining room. To her chagrin, James's place at the counter was empty and there was money laid beside his still-steaming coffee cup.

She delivered the orders and detoured past the counter to pick up the change and put his cup in the wash. Under the edge of the saucer was a hastily scrawled note on a napkin. All it said was "Later."

The breakfast crowd had left and lunch hadn't yet gotten into full swing when Lillie saw James returning.

He greeted her with an apologetic smile. "Hi. Sorry I had to leave so abruptly. My secretary, Mary June, beeped me on church business."

Lillie assumed he wouldn't have run out of the café without a word to her, the way he had, unless the summons had been important. "Anything serious?" she asked.

"Serious enough, unfortunately. There was more vandalism. Somebody lit a pile of brush on fire out on the new church property. Thankfully the flames didn't spread to the forest."

"It could have been accidental. Kids messing around with matches or something like that."

"By itself I might agree, but considering all the other things that have happened, I doubt it."

She got him a glass of ice water then leaned a hip against the counter while he sat on the opposite side. "I suppose you're right. I asked Gram about the church land. She says it used to be part of the old Pike place. Are you familiar with the history of that area?"

"Only that Gumption got its name because of Annabelle Pike's courage. It had something to do with the Trail of Tears, didn't it?"

"Yes. Benge's route went right through

this county." Lillie warmed to her subject. "When I was a little girl I wanted to grow up to be as brave as Annabelle. The legend says she was a grieving mother who had lost her newborn baby to some kind of fever. In those days, before antibiotics, there were lots of illnesses that aren't fatal now." She sighed as James nodded, listening intently.

"Anyway, Annabelle had gone walking in the woods to grieve when she came across an escaped Cherokee mother and baby. She tried to help them but the Native American woman died, leaving the baby an orphan. Annabelle took it home with her and passed it off as her own child."

"Would that have been plausible?" James asked. "I mean, didn't it look too different?"

"Not really. Many Cherokees had blue eyes. In fact, the color was sometimes called *Cherokee-blue*. The army unit in charge of the forced march tried to claim the baby but Annabelle fought them off. Word is, she took on those troopers with nothing but an iron skillet as a weapon. That took a lot of gumption."

"And that was how Gumption got its name? Fascinating."

"I thought so. Still do. I did a study of the Cherokee tribe in college and learned even more. Many Cherokees were plantation and slave owners in Georgia before they were displaced and marched off to the Territories. They weren't the primitives that I had thought. They once had money and legally owned property."

"Whatever happened to Annabelle's baby?"

"Nobody knows for sure. I assume he grew up and moved away like most young people did."

"Like you did?"

Lillie smiled. "Yes. But I got smart and came back."

To her surprise, James leaned closer and said, "I'm very glad."

"You—you are?"

He settled back in his chair. "Of course. Darla Sue needed you."

Oh, that. "Yes, she did. She does. Which reminds me, I need to help her get the rest of the fixings ready for the hamburgers." She took out her order pad. "Since you never got to eat your eggs this morning, are you hungry?"

"Starved. Are there any of Miss Darla's delicious biscuits left?"

"Not this late, I'm afraid. How about a burger?"

"Fine. Whatever."

As Lillie turned to go, she was struck by how little of Annabelle Pike's inner strength she seemed to possess. One kind, misunderstood comment from James and her heart had begun to pound, her hands tremble. Not only was she not brave enough to take on the U.S. Army, she was hardly holding her own with one attractive preacher.

James had no idea what had been bothering Lillie when she took his order but he was glad to see that by the time she delivered his lunch she'd apparently calmed down. That was a blessing because he wanted to suggest they visit the church property together and he'd hoped to catch her in an agreeable frame of mind.

"More sweet tea?" she asked in passing.

"No, thanks. But you can do me one favor."

She paused. "Sure. Dessert? We have fresh apple pie."

"No pie. I was wondering if you'd come with me out to the new site and look it over? I wasn't raised in the country the way you were and I may be missing something that would stand out if you saw it."

"Like what?"

He shrugged. "I don't know. If I did, I wouldn't be asking for your help." He leaned close once again to say quietly, "Besides, we'll never convince folks we're dating if we never go anywhere together."

"Good point." She glanced at the clock. "Since this isn't Friday or Saturday, we close at two, as you know. I should be done cleaning up by about three or three-thirty. Will that be soon enough?"

"Fine. Do you want to take your car?" The moment the words were out of his mouth, he sensed her answer because the corners of her lips were lifting in a grin.

"Nope. I want to ride on your motorcycle again," she said. "It really was fun."

He gladly let himself mirror her smile. "Wonderful. The weather is perfect for a ride in the country. And this time you're wearing jeans so we probably won't cause as much of a scandal."

She laughed. "I wouldn't be so sure of that. Three members of Gram's old Sunday-school class phoned last week to ask her for details about us."

"I can guess which three."

"Probably. Although there's no guarantee I heard about *all* the calls she got. There may actually have been dozens."

James arched an eyebrow. "Dozens? I suppose we should be flattered."

"Well, maybe *you* should be," Lillie countered. "Personally, I suspect the questions were more like 'What in the world does he see in her?' rather than the other way around."

"Then they're fools," James said flatly. "I can't think of anyone who is as easy to talk to and as intelligent as you are, Lillie. The kindness of your heart shines like sunbeams breaking through the clouds on a stormy day."

"That is so sweet," she said. "Are you sure you don't have Southern roots?"

He laughed and shook his head. "Not that I know of. Maybe I've lived around here long enough that some of the local charm has rubbed off on me."

"Well…" she drawled, "I wouldn't go quite that far. I hear a person has to be third or fourth generation to qualify as a *good old boy.*"

"Which may be part of my problem," James observed. "No matter how hard I try, I'm still not totally accepted. I may never be. I know that. I just want to do my job, continue the Lord's work the way He leads me and get along with everybody as much as it depends on me."

"Scripture again?"

"Yes. Romans 12:18."

"I thought it sounded familiar."

She turned and started for the kitchen while James finished the last bites of his lunch.

He didn't really know why he'd felt so compelled to ask Lillie to ride out to the property with him. Chances were she wouldn't be able to shed any more light on his troubles than the sheriff or the volunteer fire department had.

Still, he wanted her to go there with him, to see the place, to listen to his plans for its development and to share his vision for the future of Front Porch Christian. The church deacons, elders and trustees had the final say about any expansion plans, of course, yet he respected Lillie's opinions enough to want her input.

And if she happened to say something that would help lead him to a satisfactory conclusion about his nameless nemesis, so much the better.

James smiled to himself. However their afternoon jaunt turned out, he was looking forward to explaining his master plan and listening to her views on it. She had a quick mind, a fresh outlook and was so totally honest it was sometimes a bit of a shock.

If there was anything wrong with the property or with his ideas, Lillie Delaney would tell him straight out. Of that, he could be certain.

"I'll just leave my car here, if you don't mind, Gram," Lillie said, trying to sound nonchalant. "I'm not going straight home after we close this afternoon."

"Oh? Why not?"

"Well, as soon as we finish up here I'm planning to go for another motorcycle ride."

Darla Sue cackled like a proud hen on a

nest of freshly laid eggs. "Ha-ha! Good for you, girl. I knew you'd take to that citified preacher fella. Might as well get some good out of all those years you wasted in Chicago."

"That has absolutely nothing to do with it," Lillie insisted. "Brother James just wants to show me the new church property. There was a brush fire there this morning and he's uneasy about it."

"How does that concern you?"

"It doesn't, except that I'd like to be able to help him figure out what's been going on. This is the third time there's been unusual trouble."

"That's nothing for you to be getting involved in," the older woman cautioned. "It's none of our business."

Puzzled, Lillie regarded her in silence for a few moments before she said, "I disagree. You're a member of Front Porch Christian and I'm planning to join, so that makes it our business. We're family, in more ways than one. The Bible says we're supposed to look out for each other. Right?"

"In a manner of speaking, I suppose you are right," Darla Sue conceded. "I just worry about you, that's all. I figure, since I failed with your mama and the good Lord gave me another chance with you, I should try harder."

"What are you talking about? You didn't fail my mother."

"'Course I did. Sandra never did understand about being a good wife and mother."

"We both know she did her best." Lillie couldn't help feeling a bit defensive.

"Did she? I don't know. She's comin' around, I guess, but the way she shut herself off from you and let that man insist on a divorce was a crime. A pure crime. And I told her so, more than once."

"I know you did. But sometimes things like that can't be helped. Now that I know the facts behind what happened with Daddy I can't say I blame her."

Darla Sue huffed. "Well, I surely do."

"Maybe you're being too harsh," Lillie offered tenderly. "I don't remember the exact scriptures but I do recall that infidelity is mentioned in the Bible as a legitimate reason for divorce."

"Bah. No matter how bad it got for me and Max, I never once thought of divorcing him."

Lillie didn't know what else to say so she

kept the rest of her thoughts to herself. The argument over the religious taboo on divorce was not going to be settled one way or another in the kitchen of the little café. Biblical scholars had been discussing it for ages and were still at odds.

All Lillie knew was that since Christ could forgive anything, including murder, there was no reason to conclude that He would refuse to forgive a repentant person who had made any other kind of mistake, marriage included.

That was a comforting thought. It also reminded her that although she knew sins could be forgiven, that didn't mean she was supposed to defy God by committing them.

Yes, she reasoned, she probably had been meant to return to Gumption and help her grandmother cope. And, yes, she could see a permanent place for herself in the café. However, that was where her sureness ended.

If—and this was a big *if*—she eventually decided against remaining single, she would have to be far more careful in her choice of a mate than previous generations of women in her family had been.

Just thinking about making a lifelong commitment like that gave her the willies.

Chapter Seven

Balanced behind James on the Harley once again, Lillie had no choice but to hold on to him. She loved the feel of the wind on her face, the sense of freedom that riding the rumbling motorcycle gave her. She knew she was starting to get the hang of leaning into the corners because it felt as if they and the bike were one powerful, smooth, perfectly attuned unit.

They left the highway going east at Possum Trot Road and bumped over the dusty gravel track for about a quarter of a mile before he slowed and made the final turn onto the undeveloped church property.

Up ahead, Lillie could see where a still faintly smoldering pile of brush had been pushed into a clearing. James cautiously circled it before stopping upwind.

She stood aside, removed the helmet and shaded her eyes while he secured the bike. "Why didn't they put out the fire?"

"The chief said the stumps would probably continue to burn for days no matter what they did," he answered. "One of the local farmers brought over a tractor and pushed it up like that for us. They tell me it'll be safe enough."

"I suppose so. People around here burn their rubbish all the time. As long we've had enough rain to keep the forest and the pastures from accidentally catching fire, it's okay. The county judge very seldom orders a burn ban except in the hottest, driest part of the summer."

"So I've been told."

James led the way to a high spot and Lillie followed, carefully picking her way between the tufts of wild grass and weeds to avoid lurking insects.

He finally stopped, shaded his eyes with one hand and pointed with the other. "See that flat spot over there? That's where the main sanctuary will eventually be built.

Folks will be able to see our steeple for miles."

"They sure will! I can see why you love this piece of land. How big is it?"

"About forty acres, give or take. Nothing was surveyed that well in the past, as you probably know. We're having it redone with a GPS unit so we're sure of the boundaries."

"It's out of escrow?"

"Yes."

"Is that when your troubles started?"

"No. Actually, the first thing that happened was the egging of the church and my motorcycle. At the time, I figured it was just kids messing around."

"It still could have been."

James nodded. "Yes, it could. But then there was the vandalism in the church basement the evening you and I first met. And now this fire." He raked his fingers through his hair. "The egging and the other vandalism might not have been connected but after today I'm really beginning to think somebody has it in for me."

"The man I overheard talking in church?"

"Maybe. Or maybe it has nothing to do with him. The sheriff didn't seem too concerned when he investigated the damage that was done."

Lillie shook her head thoughtfully. "Caleb Frost isn't a bad man. He's just not used to handling complaints when he isn't familiar with all their background. Most of our crime is either feuding between two people he already knows or the result of someone just passing through and not realizing what a closely knit community Gumption is. We tend to look after our own. Strangers are immediately suspect."

"Like me, you mean?"

She laid her hand lightly, briefly, on his forearm to reinforce her support when she said, "No. Not at all. I meant, transients. You're here to stay, right?"

"That's my plan, yes."

"Then don't take this so to heart. After all, you may not be the root of the trouble. Suppose someone just doesn't want the church—or anybody—to build up here."

"Why not?"

"I don't know. But it is a possibility. You've been looking at the problem from a personal angle. Think about the land, instead. Has anyone warned you not to disturb the historical aspects of the Pike place?"

"Not to my face," James said. "I suppose I could ask around and see if I stir up anything." He pointed again. "The old Pike cabin sits back in the woods over there. I hadn't thought about it until now but we might want to restore it and turn it into a teaching tool and clubhouse for the youth. Kind of bring them up to speed on the history of Gumption and give them a retreat from the formality of the church, proper, at the same time. What do you think?"

"I think that's a wonderful idea!"

"Thanks to you," he told her. "I knew if I brought you up here you'd be able to help me."

"Really?" She was both flattered and flustered.

James began to smile. "Yes. Really. Some members of my congregation are too quick to agree with me and others are never happy no matter what I say or do. I was positive, if I told you my plans, you'd be a perfect sounding board."

His grin widened. He stuffed his hands into his pockets and struck a nonchalant pose. "So, what do you think, Miss Lillie Rose Iris Daisy Delaney? Is this a great spot for a church complex or what?"

Blushing, she took a playful swat at his shoulder, barely connecting as she said, "Hush, Jim Bob, or I'll—I'll…"

"You'll what?"

She giggled softly. "I don't know what I'll do but I'll think of something creative, I promise."

He echoed her good humor. "I don't doubt that for one second. Come on. Let's hike over to the cabin and take a look at it."

Lillie followed reluctantly, scanning the rough ground. "I don't know if I should. I haven't sprayed my ankles with anything to ward off ticks and chiggers."

"They never bother me," James told her. "Haven't had a single bite since I've lived here."

"That's a shame. You've missed the charm of this part of the country if you haven't been chewed to pieces every summer like a true Southerner." Struck by the irony of the notion she chuckled. "Hey! Maybe that's it. Maybe the bugs just don't care for the sour taste of Yankees."

When he rolled his eyes and arched his brows in an exaggerated response, she laughed even more heartily.

Lillie was disappointed to find that the old Pike cabin was in such a terrible state of disrepair. The caulking between the logs was missing; the floor had fallen in and the windows had no remaining glass. Moss was growing on the moistness in the corners and the whole place smelled musty. Still, it was interesting to see the homestead again and recall Annabelle's story.

Suddenly, the hairs on the back of Lillie's neck prickled. She stopped moving and listened.

James paused, too. "What's wrong?"

"I don't know. I just got a funny feeling. Like we were being watched."

"I didn't notice anything." He scanned the woods. "It is kind of late. I should be getting you back to town pretty soon, before your grandmother sends out a search party for us."

"She might, you know."

James laughed. "Yes. I know."

Turning to leave, Lillie wasn't quite sure

of her directions. She looked to James. "I hope you were a good Boy Scout because I have no idea which way to go."

He pointed. "That way. Past that tree with the striped bark."

Blinking with concern and curiosity, she approached the gnarled oak and peered at its trunk. "Uh-oh."

"What's the matter?"

"This looks like bear sign. They use their claws to scratch the trees to mark their territory."

"You're joking, right?"

"Nope. I'm totally serious."

"Terrific."

"Well, you asked." Looking from side to side to satisfy herself that it was safe, she proceeded. "In the fall you'll sometimes see where buck deer have rubbed the velvet off their new antlers against the trees but that damage looks different. It's more of an horizontal scrape two or three feet off the ground. Those vertical marks we just saw were definitely from claws."

"I didn't know there were any wild bears left in Arkansas."

"There aren't many. Usually you can tell

if one is passing through the area by watching the cattle. They get very nervous when they smell a predator."

"I can understand that. I'm not real relaxed about it, either."

"Don't worry. That Harley of yours made enough noise that any bears were probably long gone the minute they heard us arrive. They aren't any more anxious to meet us than we are to run into them."

"That's comforting. I don't mind rescuing kittens with you but I'm not keen on making friends with bears."

"Why not? They're God's creatures, too." The dubious look on James's face made her chuckle. "I take it you don't totally agree."

"Let's just say I have great admiration for Noah."

Amused, Lillie nodded and said, "You know, I've often wondered why he gets so much of the credit. I think Mrs. Noah should definitely be admired right up there with him. After all, she shared her floating home with all those smelly animals. I can only imagine what that had to be like."

"Yes. It's a good thing for him that his wife was so agreeable." He grew pensive.

Lillie was chagrined to see James's smile fade, his countenance become more somber. "What's wrong?"

"Nothing. Not really. I was just thinking back. My wife hated animals so we never had any pets. I didn't realize it at the time but I guess I missed that kind of companionship."

"Hey, I can get you another cat if you've changed your mind. Gram has plenty of extras."

"No thanks. I'm more of a dog person. Cats are too standoffish." His smile returned. "What is it they say? Dogs have owners, cats have servants?"

"Something like that."

They had reached the clearing where the motorcycle was parked. Lillie stood back and put on the helmet while James started the engine.

As she swung on behind him, she said, "Thanks for bringing me up here. I think it's a wonderful site."

When he replied, "Good. Your opinion means a lot to me," she was glad she was already seated at his back because she knew his heartfelt compliment had made her cheeks grow far too rosy. he last thing she wanted was to have to explain to James why she was blushing like a shy teenager on her first date.

It was nearly suppertime when James dropped Lillie at DD's to pick up her car.

"Want to come in? I know I can rustle you up another piece of pie," she offered.

"No thanks. I'm going to head back to the church and check for new messages, then work on my sermon if I have any free time."

"Okay. Thanks for the ride. It was fun." She handed him his helmet and waved as he drove away.

The trip down the block to the church took mere minutes. James glanced back as he wheeled into the parking lot and noted that Lillie was already gone.

The only things waiting for him inside his office were Post-it notes from his secretary, Mary June, about recent hospital discharges and prayer concerns and one personal letter. It was in a plain white envelope with no return address and had been placed in the center of his desktop where he couldn't miss noticing it. Curious, he tore it open.

Inside, there was one sheet of paper with a cryptic note that sounded like a threat. All it said was "You don't belong here," but it left him decidedly uneasy.

James rechecked the envelope. The postmark indicated it had been mailed the day before, from right there in Gumption.

This wasn't the first such letter he'd received. The earlier ones had been marked "personal," as was this one, but they hadn't upset him enough to cause him to report them. Now that everything else had occurred, however, he wondered if it was time to turn this latest note, and the others, over to the sheriff.

He hated to do it. Perhaps the writer was simply an unhappy individual who just needed to vent. If the letters continued or the threats escalated, however, he knew he was going to have to act on them whether he wanted to or not.

Slipping that letter into a drawer with the earlier ones, he considered working on his sermon, as he'd told Lillie he would, then changed his mind. The unfriendly note and the thoughts it had generated made him unusually restless.

Perhaps it would help settle his mind if he rode out to the church property again. He'd often gone there to think and to pray, even before the real-estate deal had been finalized.

Except for the constant presence of his cell phone and pager, he'd found solitude and tranquility in the quiet of the forest glade. Being there had always given him more peace than he'd found anywhere else and right now, that was exactly what he needed.

The sun was beginning to set by the time he arrived back at the new church property. The call of a whip-poor-will broke the stillness and another answered from somewhere in the distance. Summer was definitely on the horizon. According to the locals, whip-poor-wills nested in leaves on the forest floor and never sang to each other until the last chance of frost was past.

He left his bike and walked a few paces, his eyes on the heavens, his heart and mind reaching out to the Lord.

The fond memory of Lillie lingered in his thoughts. He did like her. A lot. There was no denying that she was a very special person, a good friend. But that was all there was to it, he insisted. He was making lots of friends among the members of his congregation and she was simply one of them. It didn't matter that she was also attractive.

Yes, it does, his conscience argued. *It's not fair to her to pretend you're interested in her when you're not because it might scare away genuine suitors.*

Except that Lillie wasn't looking for anything permanent like marriage, he added, suddenly struck by the notion that that was a terrible waste. Darla Sue had been right when she'd mentioned what a great wife Lillie would make. He was just sorry that he wasn't the marrying kind. Not anymore.

He'd had his chance and he'd failed Elizabeth twice; once when he hadn't paid enough attention to her to keep her happy in their marriage and once when he'd known he should reach out to her after their divorce and tell her about his amazing conversion.

But he hadn't acted soon enough. She had been killed before he'd been able to convince himself to try to share his faith with her. The way he saw it, he didn't deserve another chance *or* another wife, especially not one as unique and special as Lillie Delaney.

Lost in thought and self-chastisement, he wandered farther from his bike. A howl snapped him back to the present. He froze, listening.

There it was again! It sounded as if a dog was in terrible pain.

Vague notions of bears and other dangerous forest denizens flitted through his mind but he ignored them and heeded his instincts as he started into the woods to follow the sounds of distress.

Lillie's lagging energy had returned full force after she'd gotten home. Looking for a useful outlet for it, she decided to prepare a donation of canned goods for the community pantry.

She didn't try to fool herself into believing she was doing it simply for altruistic reasons. The truth of the matter was she'd have to take the surplus food to Front Porch Christian to drop it off and if she hurried she might even catch James there.

"I'm crazy," she muttered as she loaded the box of cans into her car.

"Yes, you are," she answered herself with a shake of her head. Why do this now? Why invent excuses to see him again when she knew he'd probably show up for meals at the café more often than not?

Because she needed to see him? Perhaps. Although she couldn't explain why, she had an intense desire to see James, to personally check on his welfare. It wasn't sensible but then again, since when were her feelings in regard to that man sensible?

In less than an hour from the time they'd last parted, she arrived back at the church. Unfortunately, his motorcycle was nowhere in sight.

Lillie's elation faded. She knew she could leave the boxed donations by the back door but decided that the cans might make good missiles for vandals. There was no sense inviting more theft or destruction of property.

There was also no good reason why she shouldn't merely give up and go back home, except that her instincts wouldn't let her. Therefore, she decided to swing through James's neighborhood and at least drive past the parsonage on Fifth Street. If he saw her, she'd stop. If he didn't notice her, she'd keep going. It was a foolproof plan. The only thing wrong with it was that she found no sign of him when she pulled up in front of his house, either.

The residence Front Porch Christian provided for their pastor had seen better days, she mused as she tried to decide what to do next. Its wooden siding needed a fresh coat of paint, and although the lawn was neatly mowed, the flower beds had been neglected. The place definitely needed a woman's touch to bring it alive, to make it look more inviting. Maybe later, after she got more involved in the church, she'd ask if the women's society couldn't spruce it up a bit as one of their projects.

At present, however, she had other problems. Unsure of what her next move should be, Lillie pulled away from the curb and drove on.

Eventually cruising past the turn onto Possum Trot Road, she suddenly decided to stop her car and let it idle while she thought things through. She figured since she was already so close she might as well go ahead and check the new church property, too.

Logic insisted that since James had recently left that area there would be no reason for him to have returned. Intuition argued that there was nothing wrong with seeing for herself. Intuition won. She started down the dusty road.

The instant she spotted his motorcycle parked in the clearing at the top of the hill, her heart began to speed. By the time she pulled up beside the abandoned bike, her pulse was pounding so hard she could feel it jumping in her temples.

She slammed the car into Park, leaped out and held her hand near the Harley's engine. Little warmth radiated from it. How long could it have been sitting there? And where was its rider?

Cupping her hands around her mouth, she called, "James! Where are you?"

No answer came.

She approached the edge of the forest and tried again, shouting as loudly as she could.

Still, there was no reply, no sign of the pastor.

Lillie eyed the woods. If she entered to look for him herself there was a good chance she'd get lost and become part of the problem instead of the solution. There was only one sensible thing to do. She'd have to return to her car, get her cell phone and notify the sheriff that James was missing.

She pressed her lips into a thin line. Caleb was not going to take kindly to such a call and neither was James, especially if it turned out to be unnecessary.

"Father," she prayed, "help. What should I do?"

No answer came. Lillie hesitated. Maybe the wisest choice would be to wait a little while longer and give James time to return to his bike.

Patience had never been one of her virtues. Still, she took a deep breath, tried to calm herself and decided to delay her call for as long as her anxious nature would allow.

· James had continued to follow the sounds of the animal's suffering. Now that he'd had longer to contemplate the noise of distress, he was fairly certain it was coming from a dog, not a coyote. At least he hoped so.

He slowed, listened, then altered his direction slightly.

Dappled light from the setting sun was

giving the dried brown leaves beneath his feet tinges of the crimson and yellow they had displayed the previous fall.

Suddenly, the howling ceased. James scanned the deepening shadows. There, standing next to an enormous oak, was the skinniest, most pitiful-looking, brown-and-white spotted hound he'd ever seen. Its back was arched, its head drooping.

He crouched low so he wouldn't appear threatening, held out his hand and called to it. "Here, boy."

Panting, the dog whined and wagged its tail slightly but didn't move otherwise.

James edged closer, his hand still extended. "It's okay, boy. I'm not going to hurt you. That's it. I'm your friend. See?"

Still, the dog's front feet didn't budge. It ducked its head lower and whimpered as James reached for it. That was when he saw that one of its front paws was caught in the jaws of a steel trap that had been hidden by the fallen leaves!

Muttering to himself, then asking the Lord to forgive his gut-level reaction to such cruelty, he bent and forced open the jaws of the trap.

It was hard to tell how badly the dog was hurt, but it was bleeding and he suspected at least some of the bones in its foot might be broken.

"Poor old guy," he said, speaking to soothe it as he released it. "And I thought I was having a bad day."

The dog balanced unsteadily on three legs and tried to lick his face.

"Looks like you'd better not walk on that foot," James said. "If I carry you, will you promise not to bite me?"

He smiled as he slid one arm around the animal's skinny torso and felt its ribs through the skin. "I'll need to feed you, too, but first things first."

He lifted his burden and started to walk out of the woods. "All I have to do now is figure out how I'm going to ride my bike and hold on to you without wrecking us both."

Chapter Eight

Lillie had continued to aimlessly wander the open areas of the church property, intermittently returning to her car to honk the horn and continuing to shout for James until she was hoarse.

Her sense of foreboding was too strong to deny any longer. Desperately worried, she gave up and returned to her car to fetch her cell phone and call the sheriff.

Jerking open the driver's door she saw the box of canned goods on the front seat. There was no sign of her purse!

She leaned in to check the floor, then looked in the backseat, too. Had she been so befuddled, so intent on her excuse to revisit James that she'd come out without her purse? It was possible. Unusual, but possible. She hadn't been herself since that man had entered her life.

She slammed the car door. What in the world was wrong with her? Unshed tears of frustration clouded her vision. Here she was, all alone in the impending darkness with no way to summon aid and no concrete plan for helping James. Suppose he was hurt. Suppose he was lost. Suppose…

Rubbing her eyes in disbelief, she thought she saw someone or something emerging from the woods. She blinked. Stared. Her jaw dropped. Was that who she thought it was? And if so, what was he carrying?

Taking one hesitant step, then another, she saw the last rays of the setting sun illuminating his face and knew her prayers had been answered!

With no thought for pride or propriety, she squealed with joy, shouted, "James!" and headed for him at a run.

In seconds they were face-to-face and Lillie could see why his approach had seemed awkward.

There was no way she could carry through her plan to hug him while he was toting a full-grown hound dog across his chest, so she dropped her open arms and settled for a face-splitting grin. "Hi! I was worried about you."

"I'm okay, but my buddy here has seen better days." He continued to walk so she fell into step beside him.

"What happened?"

"I heard him yowling and went to see what was wrong. He'd been caught in the jaws of a nasty trap." James began to scowl. "What are you doing back out here?"

"I could ask you the same thing."

"I often come here to think. It's peaceful. Usually. What about you?"

"I had some canned goods for the food pantry and when I didn't find you at the church or the parsonage I decided to come looking for you."

"Here? Why?"

"Beats me."

"Well, I can't see arguing with providence," he said, looking relieved. "I needed a dog ambulance and here you are."

"I beg your pardon?"

"You don't expect me to try to carry an injured animal to the vet on my bike when we have a perfectly good car available, do you?"

"Well, no, but…" She eyed the dog's foot. "Uh-oh. He's bleeding."

"Yeah, I know. Poor guy. Do you have anything in the car we can use for a bandage?"

James lowered the dog partially to the ground, hind feet first, while he supported his front quarters. "It doesn't look nearly as bad as it did when I first released him but I don't want to get your car all dirty."

"Thanks." She started rummaging in the trunk. "Here's an old scarf. That should do. Hold him still and I'll wrap his foot. Even if we weren't worried about messing up my car we wouldn't want him to lose too much blood."

As Lillie began to bandage the dog's foot, she was aware that she and James were standing, bent over, head-to-head. He was speaking softly to comfort the animal. The rumbling timbre of his voice made the hair on the back of her neck prickle and gave her goose bumps.

She finished her first aid as quickly as she could and straightened. "There. That should hold him. Give me a second to move the box of pantry donations into the trunk so we have more room up front."

"Never mind. He and I'll ride in the backseat. That way we won't interfere with your driving."

"What about your motorcycle?"

"I can come back for it later."

"Do you think it'll be okay?"

"If it isn't, it isn't. That can't be helped now."

Lillie assisted him and the dog into the car, then climbed behind the wheel. She looked into the rearview mirror, caught his eye and smiled. "You're a really nice guy, you know that?"

He chuckled and twisted aside as the hound tried to lick his face. "I'm a patsy and you know it. So does every homeless animal in Fulton County."

Lillie grinned, then started the engine. "Okay. Where to?"

"The nearest vet's office."

"Whose dog do you think he is?"

"I don't have a clue. He wasn't wearing a collar and he doesn't look very well cared for. I assume he's a stray."

"Or purposely abandoned," Lillie said tersely. "It makes me so mad when people throw out their pets like so much trash. It's as if they think a domesticated animal can find food as well as a wild one can and all they have to do is drop it off in the country and forget it."

Her gaze met his in the mirror once again. "Sorry. It's a pet peeve of mine."

"I can tell. No apologies necessary. I wonder who set that trap?"

"A better question might be *why?*" Lillie answered with an arch of her eyebrows. "I know some people do still trap around these parts but I can't see any reason for them to be doing it on church property. Maybe that trap had been there a long time and was just overlooked when the hunter picked up his string and moved to new territory."

"Maybe. I'll go back later and try to find it, see if there are any identifying marks."

"Good. And in the meantime you might want to pray that we're not stopped for any traffic violations."

"Why? Because I couldn't put my seat belt on and hold the dog still at the same time?"

Shaking her head, Lillie rolled her eyes. "Nope. That's the least of my worries right now. I seem to have left the house without my purse. I'm driving your doggy ambulance without a license. If Caleb Frost or his deputy stop us, I can probably talk my way out of a ticket, but if the state troopers pull me over I may be in trouble."

She tightened her grip on the wheel. *Trouble?* Oh, yeah, she was in trouble all right, but it had very little to do with her driving. It was her pulse that was speeding, not the car. Whenever James so much as looked at her she could feel the increased pounding.

And when he smiled? When he smiled, her heartbeats came so fast and furious it was a wonder she didn't faint dead away at his feet! Now that would be *truly* embarrassing.

He'd never know how his nearness affected her or how the problem seemed to be escalating, of course. Neither would anyone else.

It was bad enough that she, herself, knew.

An hour later, James left the dog in the care of the vet and hitched a ride with Lillie to reclaim his Harley. To his relief, the bike was right where he'd left it and seemed to be untouched.

"Well, at least something went right tonight," he said, climbing out of the car and pausing at the open passenger door to bid her goodbye. "Thanks for everything."

"You're welcome."

"I hope you locate your purse."

"I'm sure it's at home, even if Gram couldn't find it when I phoned to tell her I'd be delayed. I just got distracted and put it down in some unusual place, that's all. It'll turn up."

"I wish you'd taken the time to go home and check while I was in the treatment room with…"

"Jaws," she volunteered. "I really do think that's what you should name him, especially since you rescued him from the jaws of death. That, or Lucky, and you already said you didn't believe in luck."

"I prefer to call it *providence* instead of *luck.*"

"That's an awfully long name for a dog."

James couldn't help laughing. "You have a strange sense of humor, you know that?"

He stepped back and bent to speak to her through the open window. "Thanks again. Good night."

"Good night. Be sure to call me when you hear you can bring him home and I'll take you to pick im up."

"Who said I was going to take him home?"

"You did."

He arched an eyebrow. "I did?"

"It was implied," she answered with a giggle. "Even I know better than to argue with divine providence so I'm sure you won't make that mistake. It's very simple. You said you liked dogs and now you have one."

"Know what scares me?" James said with a shake of his head and a lopsided smile. "I'm actually beginning to imagine logic behind your conclusions."

"I knew you were a smart man when I met you. Go start your bike and be sure everything's all right so I can get on home. If Gram waited up for me, she's going to be a nervous wreck."

Puzzled, James hesitated. "I thought you called and told her what was going on while we were at the vet's office."

"I did. But that was an hour ago."

"How time flies when you're having fun," James quipped. "Okay. Hang loose. I'll be ready to go in a sec."

He circled the car and approached his bike while Lillie's headlights illuminated the area where it was parked. Everything seemed fine at first glance and when he checked it over he was satisfied that all was well.

Waving to her, he mounted the Harley. When he reached for his helmet, however, it felt too heavy. He turned it toward the head-lights and tilted it for a better view of the inside. It looked like…

His head snapped up as Lillie put her car into Reverse and began to back away. "Wait!" he called, waving.

Instead of stopping as he wanted, she waved back and continued out onto the roadway.

Using what little light he had from the single motorcycle headlight, James began to pry loose the odd contents of his helmet.

It didn't take long to ascertain that someone had stuffed the greater part of Lillie's soft leather purse into the helmet. At night, the presence of an extra strap protrud-ing from the black helmet hadn't been no-ticeable. Even if the purse had been there earlier, they might not have seen it because they were concentrating so intently on caring for the injured dog.

Who would have done such a thing? Surely, not Lillie. She might have an odd sense of humor but she wasn't a practical joker. Nor was she foolish. She'd clearly been worried about not having her driver's license with her. If she'd had any inkling of where it was, she'd have said so.

He paused to think. Perhaps a passerby had visited the secluded property after he and Lillie had left, had noticed her purse on the ground and had left it with his bike, figuring he'd find it. That scenario was plausible. But why stuff it into his helmet? Why not just hang it on the handlebars by its strap? This way, it almost seemed as if someone had purposely tried to hide it.

Well, James thought, *whatever the reason, I need to take this purse to Lillie ASAP.*

It didn't occur to him until he was already driving away that perhaps the handbag had also been ransacked.

Lillie had started to fix herself a snack when there was a rap on the back door. She left her half-made sandwich, padded across the kitchen barefoot and peeked out the window. Her eyes widened. *James?*

Astonished, she jerked open the door. "What are you doing here?" Then, she saw that he was holding out her missing shoulder bag. "You found it! Thank you. Where in the world was it?"

"Up where we were parked," he said, scowling as he passed the purse to her. "You didn't happen to stuff it into my helmet, did you?"

"What?" Her brow knit and she gave him an incredulous look. "Of course not. Why would I do that?"

"That's what I thought." He stepped through the door. "Maybe you'd better check and see if anything's missing."

Lillie turned back to the table in time to see one of her grandmother's cats stealing the lunchmeat from her sandwich. "Shoo!" She waved her arms. "Something's missing all right. My snack. Are you hungry?"

"Not as hungry as that cat. Let's do one thing at a time. Check your purse."

"Yes, sir." Lillie couldn't help her annoyed tone of voice. She knew James was simply trying to do her a favor but she'd just managed to calm down after having spent so much time with him and now here he was again. Riling her up. Making her heart skip. Causing her insides to tremble like one of Darla Sue's fancy Jell-O molds. This was getting ridiculous.

She concentrated on her purse rather than pay heed to James's closeness. He was peering over her shoulder as she rummaged through her roomy bag.

Finally, she straightened and thrust the purse aside. "I don't think anything's missing. At least not the important stuff like my credit cards and money."

"How about your cell phone?"

"It's there, too." Sidling away, she put as much distance between them as the small kitchen would allow. "Everything is fine. Sure I can't get you something to eat?"

"You've worked in a restaurant too long," he said, smiling. "You always try to feed me."

"It's Southern hospitality," Lillie countered. "We all do it."

"Well, thanks for the offer but I need to be getting home." He eyed the door leading to the parlor. "How's your grandmother feeling?"

"Fine. She was napping in her recliner when I got here so I let her sleep."

"Guess she wasn't too worried about you, then."

"I guess not." Lillie stood very still, hoping James wouldn't decide to linger and visit. She wasn't up to making any more small talk with him and the longer he stayed, the more wobbly her knees became.

I'm just hungry, she told herself. *I missed supper and I didn't have time to eat much lunch because we were too busy today.* That was it. Low blood sugar was all that was wrong with her. She didn't need James's unwarranted attention; she needed a candy bar.

A big one.

Lillie was getting herself a glass of milk to go with her second try at a sandwich when Darla Sue wandered into the kitchen. "He gone?"

"Who?"

The old woman snorted derisively. "Who, my aunt Fanny. You know very well who. The preacher."

"Yes, he's gone. Don't you know it's not polite to eavesdrop on people?"

"I wasn't eavesdropping. I live here, remember?"

Lillie was chagrined. "Sorry. I guess I'm a little testy tonight."

"So, what did Brother James want?"

"He was returning my purse. I apparently dropped it up at the new church property."

Darla Sue plunked down in a chair and leaned her elbows on the table. "Do tell. And just what were you doing up there with him at this hour? Last I heard you were at the vet with some stray."

"I wasn't with James. Well, not exactly." She sighed noisily. "It's a long story."

"I've got all night."

Placing her glass of milk across from her grandmother, Lillie sat down to eat while they talked. "Okay. You know I went up to the church land with James after work, right?"

Darla Sue nodded.

"Well, after we got back to town and I picked up my car at the restaurant, I drove home and found your note that you were next door visiting Pearl."

"So?"

"So, I was restless. While you were gone, I decided to box up some canned goods for the community pantry and take them over to the church."

"Tonight? Why not do it on your way to work in the morning?"

"I don't know." Lillie took a bite of her sandwich and chewed slowly to give herself time to think. "I guess it was just a feeling I had. Anyway, it turned out to be the right thing to do because James had found an injured dog in the woods. That's the one we ended up taking to the vet."

"Whose dog was it?"

Lillie began to grin. "I hope it ends up as James's. He needs a pet and since he's not too fond of cats, well…"

The older woman snorted. "Humph. I knew there was something wrong with him. Cats are much nicer than dogs. Cleaner, too."

"When they stay off the table and don't steal my snacks," Lillie countered. "Mr. Boots jumped up here and grabbed the meat out of my sandwich the minute I turned my back to answer the door."

"I warned you not to leave food sitting

out. Don't try changing the subject. You still haven't explained what happened to your purse. How'd the preacher come to have it?"

"I don't really know. When I looked for it to use my cell phone to call for help—after I couldn't locate James on the church property—it was missing. Then he walked out of the woods carrying that poor dog and we drove off in my car. When he went back to his bike later, he found my purse stuffed into his helmet."

"That's odd."

"We thought so. I suppose it's just one more funny thing that's happened in regard to the church since they bought that piece of land, but I don't suppose it's connected to the other things. I mean, who would bother to steal my purse and then leave everything in it?"

"I wonder…" The older woman paused, pensive. "Never mind. It can't be connected."

"What can't?" Lillie perked up. "Tell me. Even if it seems far-fetched."

"Well, it was quite a while back, as I recall. Remember Bobby Dean Dayton?"

"Sure." Lillie wasn't likely to have forgotten her first real teenage crush. "What ever happened to him? I haven't run into him since I came back to town."

"He's still around," Darla Sue said. "After his daddy died, his mama remarried and moved to a new place south of Serenity. He hasn't done much socializing around here since then. Still runs his cattle on the old home place, though."

"What does he have to do with the church?"

"Nothing, exactly. I was just thinkin'. Seems to me I remember that Bobby Dean had some trouble with vandals out on his family's land a year or so ago. I don't believe anything ever came of it, though."

"Really? That is interesting. Maybe I should go have a talk with him." She was studying her grandmother's expression when she noticed a twinkle in her eyes. "Are you saying that just to get me to go see him again?"

"Me? Mercy, no."

"Good, because I imagine he's married by now."

"Actually, I don't believe he is," Darla Sue said with a smirk. "No, sir, I don't believe the boy has found the right girl yet."

"That so-called *boy* is in his thirties, Gram. And in case you haven't noticed, so am I."

"I've noticed." She pulled a face. "But it's never too late. If you go see Bobby Dean, you tell him hello for me, you hear? I never did take to that mama of his but Bobby Dean is a real nice fella. Just like his daddy." She got a dreamy look in her eyes. "I was sweet on his grandpa Robert a long time ago. Bobby Dean's the spittin' image of him."

Lillie was so shocked by that admission she almost choked on a swallow of milk. She coughed. "You were?"

With a wistful smile, Darla Sue nodded. "Sure was. But then Max came along and swept me off my feet." She shook her head sadly. "Funny how things work out, isn't it? I haven't thought of Robert Dayton for ages. He passed away years ago and here I still am. Ah, well, maybe I'll see him again in heaven. I'd like that."

Lillie reached for her grandmother's hand. "You aren't planning on going soon, I hope?"

"No, honey. I'm in no hurry. It's just comforting to know I'll eventually get to see so many folks I cared about." She patted Lillie's hand where it lay over hers. "Don't you fret about me. The good Lord has watched over me so far and He's not about to quit now."

"I wish I had your strong faith," Lillie said. "Most of the time I feel like I'm floundering. Like God doesn't much care where I go or what I do."

That comment made her grandmother laugh. "From where I'm sittin' it sure doesn't look that way!"

Chapter Nine

The more Lillie thought about the prior problems at the Dayton farm, the more a possible connection with the church property made sense. A portion of Bobby Dean's undeveloped land did back up to the old Pike place. In reality, the farm and the church were neighbors. Therefore, if Bobby Dean had had trouble in the past, there might be some correlation with what had been going on lately. It was certainly worth looking into. Besides, it might be fun to see him again, just for nostalgia's sake.

She considered telling James about her planned visit to her old friend's farm, but when the pastor didn't show up at the café the next day, she decided it wasn't really necessary. There would be plenty of opportunity to get him involved if Bobby Dean was able to shed any light on Front Porch Christian's current problems. And if not, there was no need to bother James when she knew he had plenty of other pressing concerns.

As soon as she was done at work she started for the farm where Bobby Dean's family had lived for generations. A gentle wind was blowing and the sun shone warmly. Lillie rolled down the windows of her car to fully enjoy the weather. Spring was one of her favorite seasons, as was fall. The hot summers in Arkansas were tolerable, she supposed. So was winter if a person didn't have to go out in the ice and snow that occasionally punctuated the colder months.

Now that she'd spent years living and working in a big city she was far more aware of the pristine beauty of the Ozarks that she had once taken for granted. Yes, there were still birds and butterflies and flowers in Chicago but seeing the same kinds of things in Gumption was akin to putting just the right gilded picture frame around a masterpiece.

Heading down Highway 17 she was struck by how little that area had changed since she'd been gone. The barn at the old Perkins place had lost a little more of its corrugated tin roof every winter for as long as she could remember, yet it was still standing. Farm ponds along the road were full, thanks to the spring rains, and the fields were beginning to green up.

She slowed. The wrought iron arch over the driveway leading to the old Dayton house was rusty. Wild blackberry vines had been allowed to crowd both sides of the entrance but Lillie could tell the drive was still being used.

She made the turn and started down the narrow track, taking care to stay in the ruts so she wouldn't scratch the sides of her car on the overgrown brush. Oak and walnut limbs arched over her, making it seem as if she were driving through a tunnel of lacy greenery.

Then, the trees parted and she broke through to the open area that surrounded the farm buildings. The house was just as she remembered it, although in serious need of a fresh coat of paint. Except for an arching yellow forsythia bush in the flower bed that fronted the raised wooden porch, the whole yard could use a bit of TLC, too, she mused.

Still, seeing the place again brought a wave of melancholy. She and Bobby Dean had made some sweet, innocent, youthful memories together, hadn't they? Too bad his mother, Neva, had always treated Lillie as if she didn't belong there. What a relief it must be to the poor man to finally be free of so much unwarranted interference.

Lillie made a face as she recalled her teenage angst. To be fair, she supposed her own parents' lack of attention during that formative period of her life had made Bobby Dean's troubles seem worse than they really were. However, there was no doubt that his mother's unfriendliness had made her feel decidedly uncomfortable.

Sighing, Lillie climbed out of the car, smoothed her ruffled hair and started toward the front door. It opened as she reached the bottom of the stairs and a mature, rather good-looking man stepped out. Like Caleb Frost, there was a whole lot more of him than there had been when they were younger, but in his case the added weight looked good.

She shaded her eyes, looked up at him and smiled. "Hello, Bobby Dean. Remember me?"

"Lillie? Is that you?"

Hurrying down the steps, he swept her up in a welcoming embrace and twirled her around twice.

When he set her back on her feet, she was breathless. "Whew! I guess you do remember."

"'Course I do. I'd heard you were back in town but I just hadn't gotten around to goin' to see for myself. You look wonderful. How've you been, Lillie?"

"Good. And you?"

"Just fine." He eyed her quizzically. "This isn't a social call, is it?"

"Not exactly. If you have a few minutes I'd like to ask you about the vandalism Gram says you had around here a while back."

"Sure thing. Let's go sit up on the porch the way we used to."

Her eyebrows arched and she hesitated. "Not *exactly* the way we used to, okay?"

That made him laugh. "No, not that way. I don't think my fiancée would approve."

"You're going to get married? Oh, Bobby

Dean, I'm so happy for you! Who's the lucky girl?"

"You don't know her. We met in Ravenden when I was delivering some steers over there and we just hit it off from the start. Her name's Melinda."

"What does your mother have to say about all this?" Lillie asked cautiously.

"Actually, I haven't told her yet. I haven't told anybody in Gumption. You know Mom. The minute I get interested in somebody, she's full of reasons why it won't work. I figure I'd better tell her soon, though, before she hears it through the grapevine. I expect she'll hit the roof no matter what."

Lillie laughed and nodded. "No doubt. But don't let her ruin it for you. You deserve to be happy. You always were a great guy."

He had accompanied her onto the porch while they talked and he gestured to the porch swing. "How about it? One more swing?" He blushed. "I promise to behave myself."

Chuckling, she sat down and patted the space beside her. "I wouldn't have it any other way."

* * *

By the time Lillie had finished chatting with her old boyfriend, stopped at the market and the post office and then returned to her grandmother's house, she was running about thirty minutes behind the fresh rumors that her visit to the Dayton farm had stirred up.

Darla Sue was hanging up the telephone when Lillie walked in and set a bag of groceries on the kitchen table.

"I hear you went to see Bobby Dean."

"Already?" Lillie made a disgusted-looking face as she started putting the perishables away. "Glad to see the folks in Gumption are as observant as usual. What all did they say?"

"Oh, not much. Just that you were seen driving up to the Dayton house and you stayed a long time."

"I hope they also mentioned that Bobby Dean and I sat out on the porch instead of going inside."

"Can't say as they did. Did you?"

"Of course we did. As Brother James says, we didn't want to give any appearance of doing something wrong."

"Good for you. There's enough bad stuff

gets made up around here without really doing any of it." She helped put away the last of the groceries. "So, what did you learn? Anything helpful?"

"I'm afraid not." Lillie sighed. "Bobby Dean never did solve the riddle of who was causing him grief and all of a sudden the trouble stopped. He has no idea why."

"Too bad. What're you going to do next?"

"Me? Take off my shoes and change my clothes and maybe kick back and read a good book for a while," Lillie said. "I'm through worrying about other people's problems. It's hard, thankless work and all I seem to be able to do successfully is start more idiotic rumors."

And maybe, after she'd unwound and had a bite to eat, she'd visit James at the parsonage and fill him in on what she'd been doing to try to help. Not that it would do much good. But she hadn't seen him all day and she was kind of worried as to why he hadn't come into the café at least once, as he usually did.

One thing was certain, she told herself firmly. She was not going let the current gossip involving her expand to include him and possibly harm his ministry. Their personal situation had ceased to be funny, and it was high time they stopped purposely fueling the rumor mill.

Somehow, she was going to have to manage to drop by James's house without anyone noticing. In a place like Gumption that was probably an impossible goal but she was going to give it her best shot just the same.

James was sitting on his front porch and working on an upcoming sermon on his laptop computer when he saw Darla Sue's car drive up.

He closed the laptop, set it aside and stood to greet her. As she got out of the car and approached, head down, feet sort of shuffling, he sensed that something was amiss, though he couldn't quite put his finger on what was wrong.

He met her at the base of the porch steps and held out his hand in greeting. "Hello, Mrs. Howell. What brings you to…"

Her head tilted up so he could see her face more clearly. His eyes widened. He couldn't believe it. His caller was *not* Darla Sue

Howell. It was Lillie, wearing a curly gray wig and her grandmother's long, bulky wool coat. "What in the world are you up to?"

She laid an index finger across her lips and said, "Hush, Jim Bob. Don't blow my cover."

James began to smile, then grin, then laugh. "You're in disguise? Why?"

"Because I don't want to encourage any more rumors about you and me," she said quietly. "And I wanted to bring you up to speed on some digging into the past that I did today." She glanced from side to side as if expecting to be accosted or unmasked at any second.

"Whose past? What are you talking about?"

"It's a long story." She pulled a face. "I seem to be saying that a lot lately. Sorry. Can we go up on the porch and sit down to talk? I feel really silly standing here dressed like this."

"Sure." He considered agreeing with her assessment. Instead, he held his peace and fell in behind her, still chuckling. "Where did you get the gray hair?"

"I bought this wig for Gram when she

was so upset about her real hair growing out so slowly. She's never worn it so I thought someone should get some good out of it. Besides, I didn't know how else to come see you without stirring up the whole neighborhood."

"You could have just phoned," he said wisely. Lillie's head snapped around. The astounded look on her face told him she hadn't even thought of doing so.

"Never mind," James said, still amused. "It's usually better to air things in person so you can gauge a person's mood as they speak. That's why e-mails are so often misunderstood." He guided her to a metal porch chair. "How's this?"

"Fine. Thanks." She carefully arranged the coat over the knees of her jeans and clasped her hands in her lap. "As I said, I did some digging this afternoon. I was going to tell you about my plans ahead of time but you didn't show up at DD's today."

"I intended to. I got busy in the morning, then had a meeting with Logan Malloy, the pastor over in Serenity. When he heard I needed to go pick up Jaws, he offered to drive me."

"Oh, good. How is he?"

"Who? Logan or the dog?"

"I meant the dog." Lillie peered around him, scanning the porch. "More importantly, *where* is he?"

"Inside, sleeping on the new bed I bought him. The vet said to keep his bandaged foot as dry as possible. I thought he'd do better living in the house, at least for the time being."

Lillie smiled. "I'm glad you decided to keep him. He's just what you need, you know."

"I'll reserve judgment on that. So, what else is new? You said you were digging. Did you find out anything that will help me protect the church and its property?"

She shook her head. "Unfortunately, no. The man I went to see had had similar problems a year or so ago but he couldn't think of anything special to tell me."

"That's too bad." James couldn't help continuing to grin at her. "What did he think of your gray hair?"

Lillie colored. "Oh, I didn't wear this when I went to see Bobby Dean. After I got home and found out that the rumors were already flying about me, I decided I should try to protect your reputation."

"I thought we were going to let the busybodies talk."

"There's a limit. Besides, since they obviously think Bobby Dean and I are getting involved again, adding you to the mix would make me look—I don't know—desperate, maybe?"

"Involved *again?* Were you and he once a couple?" To James's surprise that notion didn't sit well with him.

"A long time ago. Back in high school," Lillie insisted. "That's neither here nor there. The point is, his property lies alongside the portion of the old Pike place which is now church land. When I first heard about his problems I thought he might be able to tell me who or what was at the bottom of everything."

"And he couldn't?"

"No." She shook her head soberly. "The vandalism at his place stopped as quickly as it had started."

"How strange."

James was staring off into space and pondering what Lillie had just said when he noticed a dusty red pickup truck pulling to a stop behind Darla Sue's parked car. "Hmm. This is turning into a busy evening. Looks like I have more company."

Lillie gasped as a broad-shouldered man wearing jeans, a plaid western-style shirt and a baseball cap got out and strode purposefully toward the house. "Oh, no!"

"What's wrong?"

She ducked, pulling the coat's collar up to hide her cheeks and hunkering down in the chair. "That's him!"

"Who?"

"Bobby Dean." She moaned. "I'm never going to live this down. Not in a million years."

James wasn't sure whether to laugh or take her seriously. He decided to meet the man halfway up the walk and stall until he made up his mind what to do.

He jogged down off the porch and extended his hand. "James Warner. How can I help you?"

The other man shook hands heartily. "Bobby Dean Dayton. You're the pastor of Front Porch Christian, aren't you?"

"Yes, I am."

"Good. I understand we have a mutual friend. Do you know Lillie Delaney?"

Struggling to keep a straight face, James nodded. "I certainly do. Why?"

"Because Lillie came to see me today. After she left I got to thinking. I may have an idea why I had problems before and you're having them, now."

"Really. Well, in that case, why don't you come on up and we'll talk?"

Bobby Dean peered past him at the small, shadowy figure seated alone on the porch. "I wouldn't want to interrupt."

"Believe me," James said, quirking a smile, "my other visitor will be delighted to see you."

"You're sure?"

"Positive," James said. "Turns out we're all here for the same reason."

Lillie couldn't believe that James would invite Bobby Dean onto the porch. Not when he knew how ridiculous she'd look to the other man.

James, however, treated the unusual threesome as the most natural group in the world. He stood aside, swept his arm in a magnanimous gesture and said, "Please join us. I believe you already know Lillie."

The expression on Bobby Dean's face was a cross between shock and glee. He laughed aloud. "Oh, yeah. I know her. She looked a mite better the last time I saw her, though. I guess our visit must have been harder on her than I'd thought. She's really aged since then."

Lillie twisted her mouth into a sarcastic quirk. "I'm in disguise, okay?"

"Could've fooled me," Bobby Dean said. "I thought you were just having a bad hair day."

James was clearly enjoying her discomfiture so she included him in her disgusted glance. "Very funny. Both of you. I go out of my way to keep from generating any more stupid gossip and this is the thanks I get."

"We're all grown up," Bobby Dean said, pulling a metal chair closer so they could talk more privately. "You don't have to sneak around the way we had to when we were kids. My mother's not in town and your grandmother won't care."

This was the first time Lillie had considered her charade to be childish. "It was a joke, all right? I know very well I don't have to sneak. I just didn't want to cause Brother James any more grief."

Bobby Dean arched an eyebrow at her. "Well, well. Seems like you're a lot more worried about him than you were about me. Kind of makes me think there is something going on between you two."

"Only to keep the matchmakers off our backs," James interjected. "We thought it might simplify our lives if folks thought we were interested in each other. Right, Lillie?"

She nodded. "Right." Leave it to him to be sure he stayed unattached. Well, fine. She wasn't interested in him, either, not really, in spite of her eagerness to be with him, to talk to him, to simply know he was okay. It was perfectly natural for her to be concerned about him when there was somebody bent on causing him trouble. As a resident of Gumption, she had a duty to help all its citizens. Small towns really were like a big family, even if they did have their share of dysfunctional members.

"So," James said, addressing the other man, "what can you tell us that we don't already know?"

Bobby Dean shrugged and leaned closer, his elbows resting on his knees, his hands clasped between them. "I'm not sure. It's just that I was having all my problems with vandalism at the time when I was making arrangements with some loggers to clear a portion of my land. I thought, if your plans included reduction of the forest acreage, that might make a difference. What do you think?"

Nodding, James said, "Maybe. Go on."

"There's not a lot more to it. The thing is, the attacks stopped once I'd decided not to do any clearing after all."

"Really? Hmm." Lillie was definitely interested. "You don't suppose somebody doesn't want the forest disturbed, do you? I mean, I can understand that in a way. I always hate to see beautiful old trees cut down, even if it does give the younger ones room to mature."

"I don't know," Bobby Dean said. "All I do know is, once I cancelled my plans to log it off, I didn't have any more trouble."

"We aren't going to log," James said, frowning. "All we want to do is build a bigger church."

"Then why do you need so much acreage?"

"We may add things later, such as low-cost senior housing and recreational areas." James looked to Lillie. "Could it be that simple?"

She was shaking her head. "I doubt it. I keep thinking of other things, like the old stories of buried Cherokee treasure on the Pike place, or the gold the Confederate soldiers stole from the Union forces and stashed around here somewhere."

Bobby Dean nodded. "Don't forget the outlaws. Their gangs were supposed to have hidden loot in caves all over these parts."

"That's right!"

"Are you two saying you think the church owns buried treasure?" James asked. "That's incredible."

"But not impossible."

He seemed thoughtful for a moment, then said, "Well, well. Maybe I should do a little more investigating. I've hiked a lot of the land but I haven't been over every inch of it. It might be worth another look."

"I suppose it might," Lillie said. "If you'll wait till I get off work, I'll be glad to go with you."

"Except that tomorrow is Friday. You keep DD's open late, right?"

"Yes. I'd forgotten about that."

"I suppose I could wait till the first of next week," James said slowly, thoughtfully. "Still…"

"I think that's a wonderful idea. After all, you wouldn't want to get lost in the woods without me to guide you."

Chuckling softly, James nodded. "That'll be the day. The way you got turned around out there I think I'd be better off by myself."

"You don't need to rub it in."

Bobby Dean also looked amused. "I'd forgotten about that. She never did have any sense of direction." He smiled. "Remember the time we floated down the Spring River on inner tubes and you insisted you knew the way home? You were off by a mile."

"Yeah, yeah. I remember." Lillie nodded a bit too vigorously because the motion made her wig slide forward almost to her eyebrows. Snickering, she righted it. "Oops. My hair almost fell off."

James and Bobby Dean both looked at her askance.

"I wish you two would stop bringing up

my faults and staring at me as if you think I'm a sandwich short of a picnic," Lillie said.

James's eyebrow arched. "A what?"

"It's like half a bubble out of plumb or three squares shy of a quilt." She sighed. "You Yankees probably call it just plain crazy."

"Oh. Why didn't you say so?"

"I just did," she replied, displaying the most forbearing look she could muster under the circumstances. "I would have thought, after having been in Gumption for a year, you'd have picked up some colloquialisms."

He huffed. "Hey, I'm just now getting to where I can understand almost everything that's said to me in normal conversation. I nearly got myself in hot water at one of my first evening services when I asked a deacon to give the closing prayer and he said, 'I don't care to.' I thought he was refusing, until all of a sudden he bowed his head and started to pray."

Lillie chuckled. "Around here, that's the same as saying, 'I don't mind a bit.'"

"I know that now. But at the time I was totally confused."

"No," she said, her grin widening. "You were plum bumfuzzled."

"I was?"

Out of the corner of her eye she noticed that Bobby Dean was nodding in agreement as she said, "You sure were. Now, if you gentlemen will excuse me, I'm fixin' to head home." She directed her smile at James. "For your information, that means I'm leaving. This wig itches something fierce and I think it's high time I skedaddled, anyway. Bye-bye."

Lillie was still quietly laughing to herself as she skipped down the steps, got into her grandmother's car and drove away.

Her last glance at the house had shown James and Bobby Dean, standing together on the porch of the parsonage and watching her leave.

They were both nice people, men she admired for different reasons. Bobby Dean had been more than tolerant and loving regarding his difficult mother.

And James? Well, James was special in his own way. He'd obviously been through some hard times, emotionally and financially. She didn't think for a second that he'd told her everything that had happened to him, at least not in depth. There had been too much pain in his eyes when he'd spoken of it for that.

What she did know, however, was enough. He'd suffered; he'd learned; and he'd survived, thanks
to his inner strength and his newfound faith. How would he have done without his belief in God? she wondered.

That question brought Lillie up short the instant she applied it to her own life. When she'd struck out on her own she'd thought she was leaving everything behind, but she hadn't, had she? In the back of her mind, coloring every action whether she acknowledged it or not, was the simple faith of her childhood. The faith her grandmother had imparted as she was growing up.

Now that she was back home in Gumption, it was as if she'd regained a crucial focus that she'd lost. It wasn't a matter of merely sitting in church on Sunday mornings, or even attending services or studies during the week. It was so much more, so much deeper, more poignant.

In spite of the way she'd shoved God to the back of her mind and tried to subvert her upbringing, He was still with her, still loving her as He always had. Her earthly parents might have forsaken her but the Lord had not.

Blinking back tears of thankfulness, she pulled to the side of the road and stopped the car, then bowed her head.

"I'm so sorry, Father. I didn't realize I had shut You out but I see it now. Forgive me? And show me what I need to do? I want to be back in Your family, where I belong."

In the deepest reaches of her mind, she sensed a presence, a soul-deep peace, as if God was assuring her that she had never been out of His gentle, caring hands for a single second.

Chapter Ten

James was troubled. Sitting alone on the porch after his visitors had left, he propped his feet on the railing, leaned back in the chair and stared at the clear blue sky as he let his thoughts wander. He knew it was wrong to feel jealousy but he also recognized the signs of it. When Lillie had told him she and Bobby Dean had once been close, he had felt a definite twinge in his gut. Like it or not, he *hadn't* liked it.

He huffed. His thoughts were beginning to sound as confusing as the local vernacular, weren't they? What was it Lillie had said? Bumfuzzled? That was what he was, all right. That, and more.

Examining his heart, he found, to his

dismay, that he cared deeply about the woman who had upset his well-laid plans for the future. Lillie was intelligent, beautiful inside and out, caring, loving and so much fun to be with that he craved her company as he had no one else's in a long time.

God help me, I'm beginning to see her as a permanent part of my life, he prayed silently. *Help me straighten up, Father? Please? I don't want to hurt Lillie the way I hurt Elizabeth.*

That failure wasn't his fault, he insisted. What Elizabeth had done to him and his innocent friends was what had ended their marriage. But should he have forgiven her sooner? Tried to minister to her before it was too late?

Sighing, he closed his eyes and recalled the last time he'd seen his late wife. She had refused to speak with him on the telephone so he had shown up at her door and she had laughed in his face.

"We can still make this work," James had said. "We can get counseling."

Elizabeth had tossed her head haughtily, swinging her silky dark hair back and arching a perfectly manicured eyebrow. "Oh, get a life," she had said. "I don't love you. I never did. You just don't get it, do you? The only reason I married you in the first place was because you had plenty of money. It's gone now and so am I. Accept it."

"We took vows," he'd reminded her.

"Yes, we did. And you're welcome to honor them as long as you like, darling. Just don't expect me to do the same. I've moved on. You should do the same."

The anger he had felt at that moment rekindled and flared, making his gut churn, his fists clench once again. It was that lingering anger that had kept him from sharing his faith with her later, after he'd gotten right with the Lord. And it was that anger that continued to be a sin he couldn't seem to conquer. Clearly, he had not totally forgiven Elizabeth, even at this late date. And now that she was dead he'd never have a chance to rectify his error, would he?

He had loved Elizabeth once, and look where that had led. It was too late for him to think of starting over with anyone, especially not with someone as wonderful as Lillie Delaney. She deserved a better husband than he'd been able to be. Maybe Bobby Dean.

The thought of Lillie marrying Bobby Dean caused James actual physical pain. He stood and faced the heavens, penitent, yet infuriated at the same time. It wasn't fair. Why had Lillie and he met if nothing was to come of their acquaintance? Was God testing him?

Disgusted and unsettled, he turned away, picked up his laptop computer and started into the house. If it *was* a test, he was pretty sure he had just failed it. Miserably. His latent resentment proved it.

If he'd been a layman, he'd have been able to visit his pastor for counseling. Since *he* was the pastor, he figured the best thing he could do was either let it go or call Logan Malloy over at Serenity Chapel.

James knew that confiding in Logan was the right choice. He also knew that opening up to the other pastor was going to be one of the hardest things he'd done in a long, long time.

He reached for the phone and lifted the receiver.

Lillie had pulled off her grandmother's wig and dropped it onto the car seat beside her as soon as she'd felt she was far enough away from the parsonage. Bobby Dean had been right when he'd said her attitude was a bit childish, assuming her so-called disguise was less of a joke than it was a genuine endeavor to keep from being recognized.

Recalling the astonished look on James's face when he'd first seen her, she smiled. Showing up dressed that way had been funny, hadn't it? And they'd been enjoying the shared good humor until Bobby Dean had arrived and taken the whole scenario too seriously. Oh, well, what was done was done.

She parked her grandmother's car in the drive behind her own small compact and climbed out. Darla Sue must have been watching for her because she hurried down the back porch steps before Lillie was hardly out of the car.

"Are you daft?" the older woman asked.

"Me? No more than the rest of my family," Lillie answered, refusing to take her grandmother's negative attitude to heart. She reached for her purse and the wig, straightened with them in her hand and slammed the car door. "Why?"

"Because, because..." Darla Sue made a sound that was anything but ladylike. "If you'd told me what you were up to I could of covered for you, but oh, no, you had to go visit that preacher in my car, wearing my coat. People have already started calling, wanting to know what was wrong and why I was at his house. Why *was* I there, Lillie?"

"It was just a little joke, okay?"

"I'm not laughing."

"I'm sorry. I didn't think anyone would pay attention if you were the one seen going into the parsonage. I guess I was wrong. I just didn't want it to seem as if I was over there all the time or hanging around him too much."

"Why not? You are."

"No, I'm not." She pulled a face. "Well, maybe I am, but I have good reasons. I wanted to tell him about my meeting with Bobby Dean."

"I thought you said Bobby couldn't help."

"He couldn't, but then he showed up while I was at the parsonage and we all had a nice talk."

"All *three* of you?"

"Yes. All three of us. Out on the porch in front of God and everybody."

"Well, there's that to be thankful for." She

shrugged wearily and her shoulders slumped. "I suppose it could be worse. Which reminds me, your mother called, too."

"What's her problem?"

"I don't know. She said she needed to talk to you. Sounded pretty serious, although with Sandra there's no telling. She always did make mountains out of molehills."

"Then I guess I'd better go find out what molehill she's climbing now." Lillie bent to kiss her grandmother's cheek as she passed. "I really am sorry I caused you problems, Gram. You know I'd never have done it if I'd thought it would come back on you."

"I know." Darla Sue managed a smile. "I'm glad you're good and sorry, girl, because you're way too big to spank the way I used to."

"Thank goodness!"

Lillie was laughing as she patted her diminutive grandmother on the top of the head, then led the way into the house.

Rather than make their meeting too formal, James had suggested that he and Logan meet at the county park and talk while they walked around the perimeter. Nervous, he was checking his watch for at least the tenth time when his fellow pastor arrived.

James greeted him with a firm handshake. "Thanks for coming."

"No problem. How can I help you?"

"I don't have a clue. If I did, I'd minister to myself."

Logan chuckled and fell into step beside James as they began their amble along the park's walking trail. "That's like a brain surgeon saying he's going to operate on his own skull because he knows exactly what he's doing. There are limits in any profession, my friend."

"Yeah. I see what you mean." James kept walking, looking ahead. "This is tough."

"Take your time."

"I've never told anyone else about this. Not in detail, anyway. You know I was once married?"

"Yes."

"My wife was…unfaithful." He cited the upsetting details as briefly as possible.

"I'm sorry," Logan said when James had finished speaking.

"Me, too. But that's not what's bothering me now." James cracked his knuckles to try to relieve some of the tension. "It's not what Elizabeth did back then that's the problem, it's what I didn't do after I became a believer."

Nodding, Logan remained quiet and kept pace.

"You see, I'd had enough of her to last me a lifetime. She'd said and done some pretty awful things during our marriage. After she'd divorced me it was easier to stay away from her than it was to subject myself to more of her abuse. I guess I didn't want to be reminded of the humiliation."

"That's understandable."

James nodded soberly. "That's what I kept telling myself. Only all the time we were apart, I kept getting this nagging feeling that I should go and explain to her what a difference God had made in my life."

"Forgive her?"

"That, too. I wanted to. I honestly did. But I just couldn't bring myself to act on it. I kept insisting there would be plenty of time, later on, when I was more versed in scripture."

"And there wasn't."

"No. There wasn't. She was killed in a

traffic accident about a year after our divorce, while I was still in seminary."

"I'm sorry to hear that."

"I should have been sorrier than I was. That was when I realized that not only had I not forgiven her, I'd shirked my duty by not talking to her about the Lord while I had the chance."

"I see. And you think God was limited by that?"

"What?" James asked, frowning.

"If He wanted someone to reach Elizabeth before she died, so you think He had only you to call on for that job? Seems to me that's giving your ministry a lot more importance than it deserves."

The truth of that statement brought James to a halt. Logan paused beside him and lightly touched his shoulder. "You and I have jobs to do, yes, but we're not alone in this work any more than you were the only one who could have reached your late wife. If you think about it objectively, you may even decide that you were the *worst* one to preach to her, given your marital history."

"I'd never seen it quite that way. I suppose you're right."

Logan smiled at him. "I have my

moments. Now, why don't you tell me what else is bothering you?"

"What makes you think there's anything else?"

"A pastor's instincts, maybe. Is there?"

"You're very good at this. Okay. As long as I've gone this far, you may as well know the rest. I think I'm falling for a member of my congregation and I don't have the slightest idea what to do about it."

"She's single, I hope."

"Very single. As a matter of fact, she's always saying how much she hates the idea of marriage."

"That's interesting. Want to tell me who the lady is?"

"Not yet. Up until a few minutes ago I was convinced I was unworthy of a second chance. Now, I'm not so sure."

Logan clapped him on the back. "That's what God's grace is for, my friend. Come on. Let's go over to DD's and I'll buy you a cup of coffee."

"No. Not there," James said a bit too quickly. "Anywhere but there."

Arching an eyebrow, Logan smiled. "Ah, I see."

James couldn't help returning the other man's grin. "Knowing you, Brother Malloy, you probably do see."

"Only if we're both thinking of the same eligible lady. Lillie Delaney?"

"Yes. I understand she used to date Bobby Dean Dayton."

"I know his mother, Neva. To hear her talk about it, Lillie practically left him at the altar, although I wouldn't put much stock in anything that woman says. She has a habit of looking for the worst in everyone and then proceeding to air her opinions about it, right or wrong."

"Do you think Lillie and Bobby Dean may get back together?"

Logan laughed. "I think, if there's any chance of that, you'd better make your intentions known ASAP."

James snorted in self-derision. "Right. Assuming I know what those intentions are."

Lillie telephoned her mother at home in Harrison, got no answer and tried her cell number.

Sandra answered almost immediately. "Hello?"

"Hi, Mom. It's me. You called?"

"Yes. I hear you've been dating again. I think that's wonderful."

"I'm not dating. I just have a couple of men friends, that's all."

"But it could get serious eventually, right?"

Lillie chose to bury her doubts and stick to her usual reply. "No way. I've told you before, I'm never getting married."

"Why is that, honey?"

"How can you ask that after what Daddy and Grandpa Max did?"

"Listen. I don't want to talk about this over the phone. I'm on my way to Gumption right now. I should be there in about an hour. Wait for me?"

"You're not sick are you?" Lillie asked with evident concern.

"No. I'm not sick. I just…" She broke off. "I'll explain everything when I get there. I promise."

Lillie spent the next forty-five minutes pacing, then went out onto the porch to wait for her mother's arrival.   Darla Sue had retired early, as soon as she'd heard that

Sandra was expected, and Lillie was naturally disappointed.

It was hard to love both women and watch them purposely distance themselves from each other, but since Lillie felt she owed her deepest debt to her grandmother, she didn't argue with her decision to try to avoid conflict by making herself scarce.

Perhaps, after Lillie and her mother had chatted, she'd try to talk Sandra into staying the night rather than making the long trip home and they could all get together the following morning, when everyone was rested and more likely to get along.

A white luxury car wheeled into the drive and came to an abrupt halt. Lillie immediately climbed in the passenger seat and slammed the door. "Hi, Mom."

"Hi, honey. You look wonderful."

"Thanks." She saw Sandra peering through the windshield at the house so she explained, "Gram was really tired tonight. She's gone to bed early."

"Ah. Well, that's probably for the best since I told her it was you I was coming to see. Do you want to go for a drive or shall we just sit here and talk?"

Judging by her mother's puffy, reddened eyes, Lillie figured it would be smart to remain parked. "We can sit out here, unless you'd like to go into the house."

"No. As I said, this is just between you and me. It'll be our secret. If Mom knew about it she'd pitch a fit and I'd never hear the end of it. That's why I never told her."

"Okay. You look really upset. What's wrong?"

"I am. I have been for years. When I saw how dead set you were against marriage I should have insisted you get professional counseling."

"That's silly. I don't need counseling just because I choose to remain single. Lots of people do that."

Sandra began to weep quietly, reached into her purse and retrieved a tissue. "I know. But it's partly my fault. Your father and I set a pretty poor example for you to follow."

"Forget it, Mom. I'm fine. Lots of people grow up with divorced parents. Especially these days."

"I know." Opening her arms, Sandra enfolded her daughter in the most touching, loving embrace Lillie could remember ever receiving from her.

When Sandra finally let go she said, "I could tell you were against marriage from the time you were little, even though you didn't express it at the time. When you told me you'd started blaming your choice on your father and Grandpa Max, I knew you'd sensed the undercurrent of unhappiness all along. I should have spoken up then and told you about all the good years your father and I shared. I'm so sorry."

Stunned, Lillie didn't know what to say. She didn't want to see her mother taking all the blame but she was not sure how to soften her supposed guilt.

Lillie frowned. "Surely you can't believe that your marital problems have warped me for life."

"What else is can it be?" her mother asked.

"Maybe that I just like being alone?"

Sandra studied her through weepy eyes. "Do you?"

That was a question Lillie had been asking herself for a long, long time. Until now, she had been sure of her answer.

This time, however, she shook her head and said, "No. I don't. And unfortunately,

I don't have the slightest idea what to do about it."

When she heard that, Sandra began to sob in earnest again. Lillie patted her shoulder to try to offer comfort. "You can't drive home when you're so upset. It's not safe. Stay the night? Please?

Her mother shook her head and took a breath. "I'll be fine in a few minutes. I can't let Mom see me like this."

"Okay." Lillie was more concerned about her mother's mental health than her own. "Whatever you want." She brightened, forcing herself to sound lighthearted as she said, "Tell you what. Let's walk down to the market or the sandwich shop and get a soda pop while we talk about those happier times you mentioned, shall we?"

She was delighted and relieved when Sandra agreed.

"It'll be like it was when you were little. Remember? I used to take you out for ice cream all the time."

Lillie declined to mention that she had been in the company of both her parents in those idyllic days.

It was dark as they started off down the

street but Lillie wasn't worried. In a place like Gumption, personal safety was the least of her concerns.

As long as her mother calmed down before she tried to drive all the way back to Harrison, all would be well.

She hoped.

Chapter Eleven

Rather than wait until later in the week to explore the church property, the way they had discussed, James had decided to take Lillie out there the following Sunday afternoon. The way he saw it, the trip would give him a perfect opportunity to tell her how he felt about her, confidentially, and see if she reciprocated those feelings.

When he had told Lillie about his change of plans, she had insisted that she needed to go home, change clothes and share a quick meal with her grandmother after morning church services. Therefore, he had agreed to call for her sometime around two o'clock.

She was pacing Darla Sue's driveway at four when he finally arrived.

"I'd just about given up." Lillie smoothed the hem of her T-shirt over the hips of her jeans and straightened her bright pink nylon jacket before zipping it up. "I thought you'd forgotten me."

"Not a chance," he called over the rumbling cadence of the idling Harley's engine. "Sorry I'm late. I got tied up at the last minute."

"Do we still have time for this?"

"We'll make time."

"What about the evening service? Don't you have to be back before six?"

James nodded, knowing she was right but unwilling to pass up the chance to speak privately with her as soon as possible. "That still gives us a couple of hours." He took off his helmet and handed it to her. "Here. Climb on and let's get going."

"Yes, sir!"

He was glad to see that she was as eager to be with him as he was to be with her. At least he thought she was. Perhaps he was taking her joy too personally. Maybe she was merely glad to be riding the motorcycle again and his presence had little or nothing to do with it.

That thought sat in his gut like a stone.

He watched her fasten the helmet then felt her get on behind him. Her arms encircled his waist, lightly yet securely. He couldn't blame her for being cautious, especially since the gossip mongers had been so busy of late, but he did wish she were acting more as if their courtship was real.

The first thing he was going to do, once they were at the vacant church property and could hear each other talk without having to yell over the roar of the bike's engine, was ask her if there was a chance that she might have changed her mind about eventually marrying.

Seeing that as a possibility, with himself in the role of Lillie's future husband, had shaken James to the core. Once he'd gotten past the initial shock, however, he'd begun to actually like the idea.

His biggest concern was how *she* would take it. The last thing he wanted to do was scare her off but he also didn't want to bide his time and let Bobby Dean or some other eligible bachelor step in while he was unwisely waiting for her to be ready to commit.

He slowed for the dirt road, leaving a

cloud of dust in their wake just the same. The closer he got to the moment when he'd planned to discuss their possible future with Lillie, the more nervous he became.

By the time he stopped the Harley, he was feeling more like a gawky teenager than a mature man, let alone an experienced, God-driven pastor.

Parking where they had before, he let her get off before he did, then carefully balanced the heavy motorcycle. If it fell over, it would take several strong men to right it. He ought to know. He'd made that mistake once.

Lillie took off the helmet and handed it to him, then fluffed her hair. The sight of her standing there, windblown, with rosy cheeks, sparkling blue eyes and a bright smile, thrilled him all the way to his toes.

"Okay," she said. "Lead on. I'm ready."

"I thought we could talk a little first."

She frowned. "I thought we came here to search for hidden treasure."

"Of one kind or another," James said. "The greatest treasures in my life are the people." He reached for her hand and clasped it gently. "Like you, Lillie."

To his dismay, she began to act hesitant,

uneasy. When she pulled her hand free, he released it without resistance. "The other day, when you mentioned having had a past relationship with Bobby Dean Dayton, I was surprised by how deeply that bothered me. Personally. Do you understand what I'm trying to say?"

"I—I think so."

"Good. Because this idea is pretty new to me, too. Do you suppose you might reconsider our make-believe dating strategy?"

"In what way?"

"I'd like us to see each other for real, Lillie. Date the way other people do instead of pretending. What do you say? Want to give it a try?"

"Well…"

James was encouraged by the slight smile that was beginning to return to her otherwise sober expression. Then, before she could continue, his pager beeped.

Habit made him reach for it. The number was a code for an emergency. He took out his cell phone, flipped it open and dialed Mary June's cell number.

Listening as his secretary started to speak,

he interrupted. "Hold on. You're breaking up. I'm not getting a good signal. Give me a second to hike to the top of the hill and then try it again."

As he did so, Lillie tagged along.

James smiled back at her over his shoulder, trying to be encouraging, but he knew his expression had grown grave.

The small phone was pressed to his ear. "Okay, Mary June. I can hear you better now. Go ahead. An accident? Where?"

Listening to the details, he paused for a few heartbeats, then said, "Tell them I'll be right there," before he turned his full attention back to Lillie. "Sorry. I have to go."

"Is it bad?"

"I hope not. There's been a traffic accident reported out on the highway and Mary June says someone called asking for clergy."

"Oh, dear. That does sound serious."

James gestured toward the Harley as they retraced their steps. "Come on. Unless you want to go with me, I'll drop you off at home, first."

"Don't be silly." She faced him, hands fisted on her hips. "You'll do nothing of the kind. Either way I'd just slow you down. I have my cell phone with me. I'll call Gram and have her pick me up."

"What if she's not home?"

"Then I'll call a friend. I know lots of folks who'll be glad to come get me. Your duty comes first. Get going. I'll be fine."

Hesitating, he could tell she was not going to do this his way. "All right. I don't have time to argue about it. Promise you'll call someone? I'm not leaving you here like this unless you do."

"I'll call, I'll call." She shooed him away. "Now go. Scoot. People may be hurt and need you."

"Okay. Thanks for being so understanding." He leaned closer and gave her a quick kiss on the cheek in parting, then fired up the Harley and roared away in a cloud of dust.

Lillie smiled and lightly touched the cheek he'd kissed as she watched him go. He was a truly special man, wasn't he? She'd intended to tell him that Bobby Dean was no threat, that he was ancient history, but she'd been so totally flabbergasted when James had asked to actually date her that she'd been tongue-tied.

Well, well. This had certainly been an

interesting few weeks. First she'd learned that her former boyfriend was finally planning to get married—in spite of his mother.

And now this surprise from Brother James. Whew! Life was certainly getting complicated, wasn't it?

Still trying to decide if she should be amused or scared silly by James's suggestion that they actually date each other, she fumbled in her purse until she located her cell phone.

Flipping it open, she saw the glow of the lit panel. *Oops.* Had she left it turned on all this time? She certainly hoped not because the batteries weren't good for more than a few days and she couldn't recall the last time she'd charged the little phone.

She peered at the tiny screen. Not only was it showing that the battery was nearly dead, it wasn't indicating a strong transmission signal, either. That was not a good sign. Not good at all.

Deciding to hike higher on the hill the way James had done when he'd wanted better reception, Lillie started out. She wasn't scared; she was mad—at herself and at technology in general. In the city, locating another phone to use would have been easy. Out here, she might as well howl at the moon like a coyote, for all the good it would do her. Clearly, she *had* lived in Chicago for too long because having had so many options available in the big city had made her careless.

Well, it couldn't be helped now. If she didn't manage to hitch a ride home with her grandmother or someone else, James would miss her at the evening service and would come back to get her. She knew he would. It was just a matter of waiting patiently until someone noticed she was missing.

Opening the cell phone again she noted that she still didn't have an adequate signal. Not only that, the lit display was dimming, proving her conclusions about the dying battery.

She folded her arms around herself and sighed noisily. "Okay. Here I am, Lord. Care to tell me why You stranded me out here?"

That stupid question didn't merit a divine answer, Lillie concluded with self-derision. If anything, God should be disappointed in her for not using the brains He'd given her. Well, what was done, was done. Here she was and here she'd stay, unless she opted to try to walk back to town.

Given the fact that it would soon be dark, she decided the wisest course would be to stay put rather than attempt to navigate the rough terrain when she couldn't see very well. Better to be a little chilly than to break her leg or sprain an ankle by stepping in a hidden hole or losing her footing on loose rocks. And that didn't even take into consideration all the creepy-crawlies that were undoubtedly waiting in ambush for a taste of her tender ankles.

She shuddered. Of all the drawbacks in rural Arkansas, the biting insects had to be the absolute worst.

Except maybe for the bears, she added, chagrinned. *Bears and coyotes and...*

"Now, stop it," she commanded herself, surprised at how feeble her voice sounded with the vastness of the forested hillside as a backdrop. "That's enough, already. James will be back."

Yes, she agreed silently, *but how long will that take?*

To James's puzzlement and frustration, he hadn't been able to locate any traffic accidents, even though he'd raced along the highway all the way from Gumption to Serenity and back.

It was nearly time for the evening service to begin when he called an end to his fruitless search and wheeled into the Front Porch Christian parking lot.

There was no time to change into a suit so he shed his leather jacket and left it in his office, combed his hair and went straight to the sanctuary.

"I'm sorry to keep you," he told the waiting, fidgeting congregation. "I was called away."

Eyeing the crowd, he spotted one of the local volunteer firefighters in a third-row pew. "Ronnie, I was told there was an accident out on the highway between here and Serenity. Do you know anything about it?"

The young man shook his head. "Nope. Our pagers didn't go off. Must've been a false alarm."

James frowned. "Are you sure?"

"Sure as I can be. You know I never miss a call, specially not when I'm in town, like now."

How odd, James thought. He looked to his middle-aged secretary in the pew closest to the front and saw her shrug and shake her head.

"I just took the call and passed the information on," Mary June said. "It sounded legitimate to me."

It had never occurred to James to question the validity of the original request for his help but now he was beginning to wonder if it was just one more incident in a chain of unexplained, troubling events.

He scanned the congregation, looking for Lillie and her grandmother. Neither was present. Given the fact that Darla Sue hadn't been attending church unless Lillie had accompanied her, he wondered if she'd picked Lillie up, as planned.

More concerned than ever, James made a snap decision. He stepped up to the microphone and announced, "You'll have to forgive me. I need to leave for a few minutes. I know you're expecting a lesson tonight but let's just make this a time of sharing and praise, instead."

He signaled the choir director. "Brother Paul, if you'll lead us in a few songs and then invite folks to step up and give their testimonies, I'll be most grateful."

Amid a flurry of murmurs, James hurried off the raised speaker's platform and headed for his office to grab his jacket. It was already getting cold outside. If Lillie was still stranded on the outlying church property, she could be freezing. And that didn't even begin to address the possibility that something might have happened to her.

His gut tied in a knot. Cell phone or not, he never should have left her until he'd made sure she'd reached someone to arrange for a ride home. If anything bad happened to Lillie, he'd never forgive himself.

"Please, Father," he prayed as he gunned the Harley, hunched low over the handlebars and raced toward the place where he'd left her. "Please look after Lillie. She's so special to me that I can't even put it into words."

In his heart, he knew he'd never uttered a truer statement. Nor a scarier one.

Darla Sue hadn't been particularly concerned that Lillie hadn't come home for supper until she'd gotten a call from her friend Pearl.

"You won't believe what that preacher did tonight," Pearl had said. "There we were, all set for his evening sermon, and he up and ran off."

"What do you mean, he ran off?" Darla Sue asked.

"Just what I said. He ran off. Said something about having to leave in a hurry and turned the whole shebang over to the choir director. It was pitiful, I tell you. I got up and came straight home."

"What about Lillie?"

"What about her?"

"She was with him, wasn't she?"

"Can't say as I noticed," Pearl replied. "Why? Was she supposed to be?"

"Yes. The last I heard they were going to ride out to the vacant church property on that noisy motorcycle of his. She should of been with him when he came back to town."

"Sorry. I didn't see her. You don't suppose he went off and left her, do you?"

"If he did, he's gonna get a piece of my mind," Darla Sue said flatly. "A big piece."

"Sure you can spare it?" her friend quipped.

"'Tain't funny. Lillie might be all grown up but she's still my granddaughter."

"Sorry. I know you're worried. But she's

a big girl. You and I both know she can take care of herself."

"I s'pose you're right. Still, I'm gonna make a few calls and see if I can find out what's goin' on."

"Okay. Let me know when you locate her?"

Darla Sue hung up and immediately shot a silent prayer heavenward as she began to punch in the number of Lillie's cell phone.

It sounded like it was ringing but the only answer she got was the automated voice telling her that the party she was calling was unavailable.

Lillie's teeth had begun to chatter as soon as the sun had sunk behind the row of trees atop the hill. She'd decided to stamp her feet to try to boost her circulation. So far, it wasn't helping much.

Someone should have missed her by this time, she reasoned. All she had to do was keep calm and wait for rescue. She certainly hoped James was going to be the one to come for her because she wasn't looking forward to receiving one of her grandmother's famous lectures.

That was essentially what had caused the estrangement between her mother and grandmother. Darla Sue had difficulty treating people as responsible adults when she'd known them as children. Recalling her grandmother's strong opinions, Lillie could certainly sympathize with her mother's feelings of alienation.

Darla Sue didn't mean to come across as bossy or judgmental or unloving. That was merely her way of expressing herself. For a sensitive woman like Sandra, that kind of unyielding attitude had to be terribly off-putting, even now.

Lillie rubbed her hands together and blew on them to try to warm them. Although her light jacket was zipped all the way up to her chin, it wasn't well lined and she was definitely noticing how much colder the night air was getting. The only plus was that it was now too cold to be bothered by flying insects.

The moon had risen, giving the hilltop a silvery tinge. Having prayed repeatedly for deliverance, Lillie spent her time scanning the forest behind her, wondering what wild creatures might be watching.

An engine growled and hummed in the

distance. The sound wasn't a galloping, thumping cadence like James's bike. It was more like that of a truck.

She stilled. Listened. The hills tended to make everything echo. Turning, she peered into the forest in the direction of the Dayton farm. Was it possible that Bobby Dean was out checking on his cattle and therefore might be close by? If so, her problems were solved.

Headlights cut through between the trees, their beams acting as beacons. Lillie was thrilled! She was going to get out of this predicament without upsetting Darla Sue or making poor James feel guilty about leaving her.

"Thank you, Lord," she said as she started to hurry toward the source of the lights. "Thank you, thank you, thank you."

It did occur to her that she might be acting foolishly but she immediately discounted the notion. She wasn't like those idiotic women in movies who walked into dark rooms unarmed or ventured into dangerous situations without thinking about their own safety. This was Gumption. She'd hiked these hills as a child and was totally at home here. What could possibly happen to her?

* * *

James arrived in a cloud of dust at the place where he'd left Lillie. He swiveled the handlebars to play his headlight over the hillside. His heart fell. There was no sign of her. No sign she had ever been there.

He shut off the bike. "Lillie! Lillie, where are you?"

No one answered. The night seemed unduly quiet, now that he thought about it. No whip-poor-wills sang, no crickets chirped, no frogs called to each other.

He left the Harley and jogged up the hill. "Lillie? Lillie, answer me!"

Spotting a shiny object atop a flat rock, he bent to pick it up. It was a small, silver-colored cell phone. He flipped it open and checked it. The battery was dead.

Taking out his own phone, he dialed Darla Sue's house from memory. Assuming he'd recalled the number correctly, that line was busy.

James was beside himself. He was doing no good there, yet it was the last place he'd seen Lillie and he didn't want to leave.

He lifted his face to the sky. "Father, I don't know where she is but You do. Please,

please look after her. I don't know what I'd do if anything happened to her."

Because I care deeply for her, he added to himself. It was true beyond any doubt. His fondest hope was that he'd soon have a chance to tell her exactly that.

Chapter Twelve

Lillie used the glow of the distant lights to guide her. Thanks to the moon and a cloudless night, she wasn't hiking in total blackness.

Vines with stickers grabbed at her clothing. Hickory trees bent their flexible trunks in arches over the path. The openings were high enough for a full-grown whitetail deer to pass but in some areas Lillie had to stoop low to ease her way through.

Again, she paused and listened. Either she was imagining things or she was hearing human voices.

She crested a hill, expecting to see Bobby Dean's pickup in the next valley. Instead, she found herself looking down at a larger van.

Several men were removing boxes from the back of it and disappearing into a dark hole that she assumed had to be the entrance to a cave.

Her heart pounded. It was hard to draw a steady breath. Was this what all the vandalism had been about? Were these men trying to discourage the church development because of their own illicit use of the property? It was certainly a good possibility.

Now what? she asked herself. If she left the area, she'd probably never be able to locate it again, not with her terrible sense of direction. But what good would it do to stay here? These men, whoever they were, were not going to be the kind to politely offer her a ride into town.

No kidding. She'd be fortunate to escape unscathed if they caught her spying on them.

She'd been crouching behind a scrubby cedar tree. Now, she straightened slowly and looked around. No telling where she was or which direction led back to the cleared portion of the church property. Still, she figured it was pretty stupid to stay where she was and chance discovery.

Taking a tentative step backward, she

caught the heel of her sneaker on a tree root and lost her balance. The sound of her body hitting the dried leaves and her resultant gasp of surprise echoed as if she'd purposely tried to draw attention to herself.

A man shouted. Another answered.

Lillie rolled onto her knees, leaped to her feet and started to run blindly through the forest. She stumbled repeatedly but refused to slow down.

The voices were gaining on her. A bright beam of light swept the woods, then came to rest on her back, casting her shadow ahead of her. They knew where she was!

Before she could dodge or hide, a large hand grabbed her by the arm and threw her off balance.

The light her captor shone in her eyes was blinding. She gasped as someone slipped a burlap sack over her head.

"What're we going to do with her?"

"I don't know."

"Let me go," Lillie pleaded. "I'm always lost. I could never find my way back here again. I have no sense of direction. Honest. Ask anybody."

One of the men laughed coarsely. "Bring

her along, boys. We'll stash her with the stuff till I decide what to do with her."

Tears wet Lillie's cheeks. She was too frightened to pray sensibly. All she could do was whisper "Help," over and over again and trust the Lord to understand.

James was at his wits' end. He'd tried Mrs. Howell's number repeatedly. It was always busy. That left the sheriff as his only viable option. If Lillie had hitched a ride to town with someone else, she'd be upset that he'd involved Caleb Frost. Then again, if she hadn't and was lost in the woods, the sooner he summoned aid, the better.

Punching in 9-1-1, James waited. Nothing happened. He stared at his cell phone. The instrument was registering a weak signal, as it had before. Could that be why he couldn't reach Mrs. Howell or why Lillie hadn't called home?

Assuming she hadn't done so, he added, growing more and more frustrated and disgusted with himself.

He should have waited until she'd made her call to her grandmother. Should have insisted he take her home first. Should have used his head and done things his way instead of letting her talk him out of it.

Well, he wasn't getting anywhere beating himself up about it, was he?

Racing back to the Harley, he swung on and gunned the engine. One way or another he was going to get help and find Lillie, even if he made her mad by involving others.

The only thing that counted, at this point, was her ultimate safety.

Later, he'd apologize.

After he found her.

If he found her.

Lillie was freezing; her legs were cramped and she'd lost most of the feeling in her fingers. Whoever had trussed her up had used duct tape instead of rope and it was impossible to even wiggle, let alone work her bonds loose.

What a revolting development this was, she thought wryly. Well, at least her captors had dragged her back to their cave instead of leaving her out in the forest to get hypothermia or be eaten by goodness-knows-what. As far as she was concerned, that was a good sign. If they'd planned to harm her, they'd hardly have gone to all this trouble.

Her mind wandered to happier thoughts. Thoughts of James. He must be so worried by now, poor man. She could picture his kind expression, his sweet smile, the way the little lines at the corners of his eyes crinkled when he was amused. He was no kid but he wore his maturity well. It made him far more attractive, in her estimation, than a younger man would have been.

Smiling as best she could in spite of the tape covering her mouth, Lillie imagined herself returning the tender kiss he had placed on her cheek the last time she'd seen him. Someday, she would do it, she vowed silently. Someday, she was going to give that man the most perfect, most loving kiss he'd ever experienced. In view of her past heitancy to commit to anyone else, it was probably going to be the best kiss *she'd* ever shared, too!

But first she had to get loose and get back to him, she told herself with a shiver, and that was not going to be easy. Not only was she tied up and hidden, she had no earthly idea which way she should flee, if and when she did manage to get loose.

This wasn't a job for a superhero or for

James, Lillie realized prayerfully. It was a job for God. He'd protected her so far. He was her only real hope.

"Okay. Meet me at your house," Caleb had said when James had finally gotten through to him.

James wasn't happy with the choice. "Why not at the church property? It'll save time."

"Because I want to organize the search and give everybody orders before they show up out there and stomp all over any clues Miss Lillie might of left," the sheriff said.

"Okay. I'm at the parsonage now. It's on Fifth Street."

"I know. I was born and raised here, remember?"

"Sorry. I'm not trying to tell you how to do your job. I'm just very worried about her."

"I can understand that," Caleb said. "Shouldn't of left her there by herself. Not at that time of night."

"Believe me, I know that now. It wasn't dark when I got the accident call. Like I told you, Lillie was supposed to call Miss Darla Sue for a ride."

"But according to what Miz Howell says, she never did. I checked."

"That's what I was afraid of."

The sheriff sounded concerned. "Okay. I'll gather up some of the boys and we'll be there in two shakes of a hound dog's tail. Sit tight, y'hear?"

"Yes, Sheriff. I hear you."

It was all James could do to remain polite in the face of the other man's accusatory tone. Not that he didn't deserve chastisement. Nobody could have beaten him up any worse than what he was doing to himself.

And speaking of hound dogs... James climbed the front steps and opened the door so Jaws could join him on the porch. He ruffled the dog's silky-feeling ears as it leaned against him and begged for affection.

"You still like me, don't you, boy? Probably a lot better than I like myself right now."

The brown-and-white dog wagged its tail more rapidly in response to his voice.

James plunked down on the top step and Jaws pushed closer, half on, half off his lap. "You weren't lonesome, were you? I guess you were." He grasped the dog's front leg and lifted it to look. "How's the paw healing?"

Jaws lunged to lick his face, managing a quick wet swipe of the tongue under James's chin before he leaned farther away.

"So, you were done with the bandage, huh? What did you do, chew it off while I was gone?" He examined the hurt paw and was pleased to see barely a hint of the earlier injury. As the vet had assured them, the bleeding had masked the small cut and had made it look a lot worse than it really was.

He looped an arm over the dog's shoulders and gave it an affectionate hug. "I'm glad to see at least one of us is doing better, old boy. Personally, I've had a rough day."

And it didn't look as if it was going to improve soon, James added. What was keeping that sheriff? Didn't he know that every second Lillie was lost was one more second when she could be in danger?

He shuddered.

The dog reacted immediately, tensing and bristling as if defending his new master.

James patted him to calm him. "It's okay, boy. The only person I need protection from is me. If anything bad happens to Lillie, I'll never forgive myself."

That was true. Just as he had with Elizabeth, he had held back his true feelings for Lillie instead of expressing them in a timely manner. He supposed the comparison was unfair because at least he had tried to tell Lillie how he felt, but the suggestion, however implausible, that he might be facing the same kind of trauma and loss, gave him chills that pierced his heart and soul.

Ever since he'd discovered that Lillie was missing he'd prayed almost without ceasing. Now, spent and despondent, he found that spiritually correct words failed him.

Closing his eyes, he thought of Lillie and let his mind call out to God however it best could.

"You can't take that mangy hound along," Caleb told James. "If we decide we need tracking dogs, we'll bring 'em in from Little Rock come daybreak."

Reluctantly, James shut Jaws in the house and rejoined the men gathered on the front lawn of the parsonage. "Okay. What now?"

"We'll go in a caravan," Caleb said. "You

lead on your motorcycle and follow the same route you used before. When we get there, the rest of us will park down below and fan out on foot so we can make a wider sweep. If anybody turns up Miss Lillie's footprints, we'll go from there." He waited for nods of agreement from the rest of the men.

James mounted his Harley and swung away from the curb. Behind him he could hear the other trucks and cars starting up. Headlights shone past him, lengthening his shadow and making it repeat in multiples on the road ahead.

His peripheral vision caught movement and he glanced to one side. Loping along beside him, as if his foot had never been hurt, was the hound he and Lillie had rescued.

Not slowing, James continued to lead the procession out of town. If the dog wanted to go badly enough to escape from the house and run on a sore foot besides, he wasn't going to deny him the privilege. If Caleb didn't like it, tough.

The sheriff could turn back and take the dog home if he didn't want him there.

Nothing— absolutely nothing—was going to divert James from the search for his beloved Lillie.

Alone in the cave, Lillie had managed to wiggle her fingers and free her mouth by raising her clasped wrists and peeling off the tape. She had then spent hours working on the bindings around her wrists with her teeth.

She wasn't looking forward to the return of her captors but she wasn't keen on being the only one keeping company with the resident wildlife, either, even though the men who had caught her had left a small lantern burning so she wouldn't be in total darkness.

This part of the Ozarks was well known for its limestone caves, including some gigantic caverns that were world-famous tourist attractions. This cave, however, had a low ceiling and no visible stalactites or stalagmites.

To her right was the opening that evidently led back to the forest trail. To her left, the passageway tapered off into a narrowing dark hole that seemed endless. That was where the thieves had stacked cardboard cartons containing their booty.

If the labels on those boxes were to be believed, she hadn't found Confederate treasure or loot from outlaw robberies at the turn of the previous century. These cartons held modern electronics such as TVs and computers. If Lillie hadn't been trussed up like a Christmas goose and so cold her teeth chattered, she might have found the whole scenario amusing.

"Only this is *not* funny," she muttered. "Not funny at all."

Thinking about her loved ones, she was surprised to find that she didn't yearn most for her grandmother or her mother or any of her girlfriends. The only person whom she truly wanted to find her, to hold her, to rescue and comfort her, was James Warner. She didn't care if he thought she was too brazen. The minute she next set eyes on him she fully intended to run straight into his arms and hang on for dear life, whether it embarrassed him or not.

She didn't care what the gossips said. She didn't care what her grandmother said. She didn't even care what the rest of the congregation at Front Porch Christian said. Danger had made her see what was really important. James was. And even though it was contrary to all her previous plans, she couldn't help imagining what it would be like to spend the rest of her days with him.

Thinking about the remainder of her life brought her nearly to tears. It wasn't over. It couldn't be over. Not now that she'd finally found the companionship she'd been searching for, yearning for, for so long. She wasn't giving up. No sirree. She was going to get out of this mess and live to be ninety or one hundred, just like Annabelle Pike had.

And if it turned out that that life was to be spent with James, all the better. If not, at least he had helped her realize that she really didn't want to grow old alone.

She scanned the area that was illuminated by the small lantern. There was no frying pan to use as a weapon the way Annabelle had in the 1800s, but maybe there was something hard or heavy, or both, in one of the boxes. As soon as she was loose she'd open them and look.

Trying to control her shaking enough to take firmer bites, she went back to chewing on her tape bindings. The stuff tasted like dirt and the little pieces of silver backing came off without loosening the tough, sticky, lengthwise fibers that were the basis of the duct tape's strength.

Lillie sniffled, discouraged, but kept on working. She was not quitting till she was free.

Or until someone came back and stopped her.

"Think," she whispered. "Calm down and think."

She stared at her bindings. Chewing against the grain had gotten her nowhere. There were long, tough fibers on the sticky side of the tape. Therefore, if she could get hold of one end of any of the strips, there was a good chance she could peel them off the way she had the short piece they'd stuck across her mouth.

Peering at the silvery tape, she spotted a rough edge. She twisted her hands as far as they'd go, lifted them to her face and bit into the frayed end. It gave!

"Hallelujah!" She breathed raggedly, excitedly. This method was going to work!

James and the dog raced to the top of the hill while the sheriff and his makeshift posse stopped at the bottom. James knew he should wait there, as Caleb had ordered. He had intended to obey. But almost as soon as he'd parked, Jaws had let out a howl and veered into the forest.

The decision to follow was easy to make. James figured he was better off going with the dog than standing there for who knew how long waiting for the sheriff to get his men organized. There was a chance that the dog was trailing Lillie. James was not about to delay and allow him to get out of sight.

Grabbing the flashlight he'd brought, he started after Jaws, calling to him. The dog hesitated briefly, looked back, then took off again, baying with even more gusto, as if he understood that his new master was with him on his quest.

Keeping his light aimed at the dog's white tail, James hurried after him. He must not get away. He might be Lillie's first, best hope of rescue.

Her neck and shoulder muscles ached and her teeth hurt but Lillie had finally worked the last of the tape loose from her wrists.

Bending, she made quick work of the strips wound around her ankles.

Stiff but exuberant, she straightened and scanned the cave. Was it wise to stop and look for a weapon or should she simply grab the lantern and flee?

The idea of getting out of there was strong enough to override her weariness. Staggering, stumbling, she stamped her feet to try to increase the circulation in her icy limbs. Being so cold was uncomfortable but it was probably for the best. Once she got warmer, her strained muscles were probably going to really start to ache.

She grabbed the battery-powered lantern and swung it in an arc, looking for the cave exit. Logically, it had to be opposite the stash of stolen goods, she reasoned, starting off. Once she was outside, she'd decide where to go.

Anything had to be better than staying where she was and trusting the thieves to be compassionate to her. After all, she was probably the only outsider who knew what they were up to. Putting herself in their place and trying to think the way she believed they would, she knew she'd have been anything but understanding or lenient.

The atmosphere outside the cave was damp, humid, foggy, as she stepped into the clear. The usually welcoming forest looked forbidding. If Lillie had not had the lantern, she wouldn't have chanced venturing into the night.

As it was, however, she figured it was nice of the good Lord to have provided the illumination she needed and she was determined to put it to use.

If she got lost? Well, so what? Eventually she was bound to reach either a road or the fence to the Dayton farm. By following that lead, she could work her way back to civilization.

How long it would take or whether her lantern batteries would last long enough was immaterial. All that mattered was getting away.

The sooner, the faster, the better.

Chapter Thirteen

James almost lost track of the dog several times but its baying gave enough clues to its ongoing location that he was still able to follow.

Breathing hard, he cleared the top of a hill. Several dozen yards below, Jaws was circling, his nose to the ground, his tail wagging. Then, as if summoned by an unheard voice, he took off into the woods to James's right.

James was able to follow more easily by keeping to the ridge. He saw the dog hesitate, then change direction again, heading toward him. His heart fell. Maybe the stupid hound was merely playing and had now decided to return to him for more of the game.

James paused and bent over, hands resting on his knees, sides heaving and ribs aching, trying to catch his breath. When he straightened, he thought he saw a weak beam of light ahead. Taking a chance, he called, "Lillie?"

The beam swung his way. It was wavering, as if its source wasn't able to hold it steady. He held his breath, listening, then called again. "Lillie?"

There was a squeal. "James? James, over here! I'm over here," she shouted.

Elated, he couldn't make his feet move fast enough. Zigzagging among the trees, he closed the distance between them. He hadn't imagined it. It *was* her! He'd found Lillie.

And so had the faithful dog.

Lillie felt faint. She was so relieved, so joyful, she could hardly speak. She had been petting Jaws with great delight but when James ran up to her she forgot about everything else. Dropping her light, she threw herself into his embrace without a second thought.

He held her tightly. Arms around his waist, she laid her cheek on his chest and listened to the pounding of his heart. She could feel his warm breath on her hair. Was he also kissing her there? She suspected he was and the idea thrilled her. Clearly, James was as glad to see her as she was to see him.

Finally, she eased away and looked up at him. Even in the dimness of the moonlit woods, she could see his eyes glimmering with unshed tears. Hers were wet, too. She smiled and managed to utter a faint "Hi."

"Hello," he said hoarsely, "I'm glad to see you."

"I can tell," Lillie answered. "I'm pretty glad to see you, too."

"What happened? Where were you?"

"It's a long story," she said, suddenly aware that they might still be in danger of discovery. "We need to get out of here." Her smile widened to a grin. "Any idea of which way is out?"

"Back that way," he said, gesturing with a nod. "The sheriff is here, too. I had to call him. I couldn't take a chance that you were in real trouble."

Slipping one arm around his waist, she stepped to his side and urged him in the direction he'd indicated. "Good. We'll need

Caleb. Let's get back. I have plenty to tell him."

"About what?"

"I think I stumbled on the reason why you've been having so much trouble out here," she said.

"Okay. What's the hurry?"

"I'll explain it all when we're safely with the sheriff. I don't want to get caught again."

"Again?" His hold on her tightened.

"It's okay. I'm fine now that you're here and I'm not lost anymore." She continued to tug at him. "Move, Jim Bob. These woods are not as safe as they look."

She sensed him giving in. He fell into step beside her, grasping her hand and staying close in spite of their difficulty maneuvering in and out of clumps of trees and brush as a couple. Lillie was glad. She didn't want to let go of him, either, and it was all she could do to keep from stopping to give him another hug. And another. And another.

She smiled to herself, glad the darkness kept some of her poignant sentiments secret. When they were back in the light of day and all the excitement had died down, James might not feel quite as affectionate toward her as he did now and she didn't want to cause him undue embarrassment.

Presently, however, she was more than happy to take advantage of his closeness, his strength, his gentle compassion. Even if she'd been imagining things and he wasn't really ready for a romantic relationship, she'd have this moment to remember and cherish.

And if he was prepared to get serious about courting her, as she'd thought he'd been trying to say before he'd been called away? What then? Was she really ready for that or was her imagination making more of his words than it should be, simply because she'd experienced a bad fright?

Lillie didn't know. Nor was she going to worry about it. As long as James was holding her hand and leading her to safety, that was enough of an answer to prayer to suit her.

She didn't know where it was written but she was sure she recalled that the Bible said, "The cares of today are sufficient for today."

Therefore, tomorrow would take care of itself. And if James was no longer eager to date her after all the worry she'd caused him? What then?

Sobering, Lillie held tighter to James's hand and silently prayed that he hadn't changed his mind.

After Lillie and James had returned and reported to Caleb, he and his posse had waited till daybreak, then begun to search the woods.

Lillie couldn't tell them exactly where she'd been held but James had been able to give an approximate direction and that had been enough to ensure their success.

Lillie was at home with her grandmother when James dropped by later to tell her what had transpired.

Darla Sue met him at the backdoor and stood in his way. "She's resting," the elderly woman said.

"I understand," James answered gently. "But I know she'll want to hear what the sheriff found."

Reluctantly, Darla Sue stepped aside. "Okay. I guess you can come in."

"Thank you."

"She wouldn't of been in that fix in the first place if you hadn't gone off and left her."

James was duly ashamed. "You're right. And I apologize. When Lillie promised to call you for a ride home I never dreamed she wouldn't be able to get through."

"Her stupid phone was dead, I reckon," Darla Sue said. "You should of checked."

"I know I should have. If it helps, I feel terrible about it."

"Good. Leavin' that poor girl out there like that was clear criminal."

"Speaking of criminals, did Lillie tell you what she discovered?"

"She did. Is the sheriff doing his duty?"

"He's working on it right now," James said. He looked up as Lillie entered the kitchen and his heart sped. Her hair was mussed and she was dressed in a faded blue sweatshirt and pants but she had never looked prettier to him.

"Hi there." Yawning and stretching, she smiled. "Sorry. I've been napping."

"You deserve the rest," he said. Looking to Darla Sue, he asked, "Did you close the café today?"

"Nope. Never have missed a day of business and never will, long as I have any say in the matter. Rosie's cookin' and Helen and

Ruth Ann are handling the front. They'll muddle through till Lillie and I can go back to work."

Lillie's eyes widened. "You didn't have to stay here with me, Gram. I'm fine. Honest."

The older woman raised a gray eyebrow and glared at James. "Looks like it's a good thing I stayed home, what with him comin' over like this. There's plenty of talk about you two bein' out all night as it is."

James spoke up. "We weren't together after dark, except when I was leading Lillie out of the woods. With the sheriff and his men all over the place, I can't see how anyone would think we were up to anything illicit."

"Humph."

Lillie began to giggle. "You might as well give it up, Jim Bob," she said with a shake of her head. "You're never going to please everybody in Gumption, especially not folks who want to gossip."

"I guess not. I'm just sorry your reputation is suffering."

"I'm not worried about that," she said. "What I want to know is whether Caleb found the loot."

"He did. Last I heard, he was tracking down the thieves. I guess our problems are over."

"I guess so."

James glanced at Darla Sue out of the corner of his eye, then concentrated on Lillie. "Can we go out on the porch for a minute? I'd like to talk to you."

"There's nothin' y'all can't say in front of me," the older woman insisted.

"Gram? Please?"

"Oh, all right. You and the preacher sit down right here and have a cup of coffee or something. I'll be in the living room, knitting and minding my own business."

Lillie chuckled and kissed her grandmother's cheek as she passed by. "Thanks. You're a dear."

"Bah. Considering the poor judgment you've been showin' lately, I won't be goin' far."

James was also smiling. He knew he was looking at Lillie with more affection than he had any right to, but he was so relieved that she was safe and sound he couldn't help himself.

She crossed to the percolator and lifted it. "Coffee? It feels like we have plenty made."

"That'll be fine. Thanks."

As she brought their steaming mugs to the table, he held a chair for her.

"You're going to spoil me," she said, sliding into the seat.

"I certainly hope so." He chose the closest empty chair for himself. "How are you feeling? Really."

"Stiff and a little sore, but otherwise fine," Lillie answered. She passed him one of the mugs. "I've been sleeping since I got home. What time is it, anyway?"

"Afternoon," he answered. "I came by to tell you that the sheriff found the exact place where you were held." He reached for her hand where it lay on the table, his thumb gently caressing her wrist. "The torn duct tape was right where you'd left it. And the other stuff in the boxes had been stolen, just as you thought."

"So, that settles it?"

"As far as Caleb is concerned, yes. It's hard for me to believe it's that simple, but I guess it is."

She smiled at him. "In case you haven't made the connection yet, if you hadn't left me up there where I could see the lights in the woods, we still wouldn't know what had been going on."

"I'd rather not know than take a chance on having you hurt."

"Thanks." She squeezed his fingers. "But it did turn out all right."

"No thanks to me," he said with self-derision. "I can't believe I left you the way I did. It was unforgivable."

"Suppose you let me be the judge of that. After all, I could have stayed put and waited for you to miss me and come back for me. I had intended to, until I saw the glow coming from over the ridge. Waiting would have been the most sensible thing to do."

James laid his other hand over hers and searched her gaze, looking for the same depth of emotion he was feeling. "I meant what I said right before I got the page to go to the accident scene." His words sounded throaty, poignant. "I would like to start seeing you. Dating you. If that's all right."

She merely nodded. He could tell she was touched.

"And I don't care what anyone else says," James went on. "You and I are all that matters."

"If…if it works out. I can't promise

anything," Lillie said with obvious hesitancy. "This whole concept of a serious relationship is new to me."

James smiled. "Yeah. Me, too. You'd think, at our ages, we'd have the kinks worked out, wouldn't you?"

"I don't think age has as much to do with it." Lillie said. "We both have our excess baggage, so to speak."

"I'm okay with that if you are."

He was afraid for a moment that she wasn't going to agree.

When she finally said, "So am I," his heart leaped.

He knew he'd have to take it slowly in order to keep her from changing her mind but he didn't care.

As long as there was a chance for them to find happiness together he was willing to do whatever it took to bring that about.

Lillie had wondered why James had not kissed her goodbye when he'd left. He'd sounded sincere and he'd acted as if he cared for her, yet he'd made no move to embrace her again or even kiss her on the cheek when she'd walked him to the door.

Should she have made the first move? she wondered. Maybe he was just shy. Then again, maybe he was being chivalrous.

The way she'd felt lately was anything but subdued with regard to that man, but then, what did she know about the way men's minds worked? If she had acted on her urge to throw herself into his arms and kiss him senseless, the way she'd wanted to, he might have run like a scared rabbit.

The mental picture made Lillie smile. Mere weeks ago, if anyone had told her she'd be considering throwing herself at any man, let alone a preacher, she'd have laughed in their face. She wouldn't blame James if he ran scared as a result, either, considering the way other single women had been so overt in chasing him.

There had never been a man like James in her life and she didn't want to lose him. He was different from anyone she had ever dated. Not absolutely perfect in the human sense but more than perfect for her. The only thing that truly worried her was how she should act when she was around him.

Lillie drew in a deep breath and released it as a sigh. "I need to be myself," she insisted. "If I knew who I really was, that might not be so hard to do."

And now I'm talking to myself, she added silently. *Terrific. Just one more quirk to add to my already sterling personality.*

The thought amused her enough to generate a giggle. Darla Sue overheard and joined her in the kitchen.

"He gone?" she asked.

"Yes. He left a few minutes ago."

"Well?"

"Well, what?"

"Are you two goin' steady or not?"

"That's for teenagers, Gram. Let's just say that James and I plan to start seeing each other socially."

"Bah. Sounds way too formal to me. Do you cotton to him, girl?"

"You could put it that way." Lillie knew she'd started to blush because her cheeks felt far too warm.

"Did you tell him?"

"Not in so many words. But I think he understands how I feel."

"Ha! It's not like talking to you or me. He's a man. You've gotta spell it out for most of 'em."

"I don't want to scare him away."

"You've got it that bad?"

Lillie shrugged. "Could be."

"Then if I was you, I'd tell him before he changes his mind," Darla Sue warned.

"If he cares for me, he's not going to change his mind, is he?"

"Can't say. He might. I told you about me and Robert Dayton, all those years ago. After I met Max, Robert got real jealous. I thought it was fun to keep two men on a string. Turned out it was the dumbest thing I'd ever done. Nearly lost 'em both while I was playin' games."

"Have you heard from Grandpa?" Lillie asked. She hadn't expected an affirmative answer so she was shocked when her grandmother nodded. "Yeah. He'll be home in a few more days."

Lillie froze. "He's coming home?"

"So he says."

"Then I have to leave."

"You'll do nothing of the kind," Darla Sue insisted. "This is my home and I want you here. Max'll just have to adjust if he wants to move back in with us."

"No. That's not right. I caused problems

between you two in the past, when I was too young to realize I was doing it. I'm not going to make that mistake again."

"Where'll you go?"

"I don't know but I'm not staying. Having me here will make it much harder for you and him to talk openly, to settle whatever is between you. I'm sure I can find a little place to rent close by."

"All right, but don't you sign a lease, you hear? I'm not sure your grandpa is going to stay, if you get my meaning."

"You're not going to forgive him this time?"

"I don't know," the older woman said. Her shoulders slumped. "I'm tired, girl. Maybe too tired to fuss with patching things up between me and Max. We'll have to wait and see."

Lillie stepped closer and gave her grandmother a hug. She could feel bones through the woman's sweater. Darla Sue was getting frail, far more frail than she'd ever admit.

As her only close relative, barring a successful reunion with Max, she owed it to her grandmother to protect her, to stand up for her, no matter what.

Yes, she'd still look for a place in Gumption to rent. If she couldn't find one, however, she'd take that as a sign that the good Lord wanted her to be with Darla when Max finally came home.

It wasn't a confrontation Lillie was looking forward to, yet she saw no way to avoid her familial responsibility. Either she'd been brought there to protect and assist her dear loved one, as Darla Sue had suggested from the start, or she hadn't.

The more Lillie thought about the situation, the more she was convinced that her presence had been divinely orchestrated. Who was she to argue with God?

And if she'd come to Gumption merely because she was destined to meet James? That notion made her smile and expand her horizons. Considering carefully, she came to the logical conclusion that God was capable of accomplishing more than one thing at a time. What a concept!

Chapter Fourteen

James waited until the following day to try to telephone Lillie. When there was no answer at the Howell residence he immediately headed for the café.

The instant he entered and saw her, he felt his heart begin to beat faster. He hurried across the checkerboard-tiled floor and took his regular seat at the counter.

Grinning, she joined him. "Hi. Long time no see."

"Too long," James said. He reached for her hand and noticed bruising on her wrist. The thought that she'd been hurt because of a poor decision he'd made pained him deeply.

His thumbs caressed the injured place while he gently held her hand. "I'm so, so sorry."

"Quit beating yourself up, Jim Bob. Nobody's perfect. You did what both of us thought was right." She continued to smile at him. "You never did tell me. Who was in the accident you went to?"

He began to frown. "There wasn't one. At least not that I could find. And by the time I gave up looking, it was time for the evening service."

"How odd." Her brow knit, too. "I wonder who put in the original call."

"I don't know. Mary June says she didn't recognize the caller's voice. I suspect the accident report was meant to draw me away from the church property."

"Only the bad guys didn't expect me to stay behind?" Lillie finished for him. "I suppose that is plausible."

"Unfortunately. Well, at least the vandalism should be over now."

"Did the sheriff make any arrests?"

"Yes. Several. He says he got all the crooks."

"Good." She tugged her hand free and reached for her order pad and pencil. "So, did you come here to visit or are you hungry, too?"

"I'll gladly eat if that's what it takes to get

you to stand here and talk to me," James said with a smile.

Lillie laughed lightly. "In your case, I'll make an exception. You don't have to eat anything if you don't want to. I'm just glad to see you."

"Me, too," he said, pretty sure he was blushing. "You aren't worried about tarnishing your reputation?"

"By keeping company with you? Not hardly. Which reminds me. Gram and I would like to invite you for supper."

"I'd be delighted. When?"

She sobered. "Thursday, I think. Maybe you won't want to come when you hear who else is supposed to be there. Max is coming home. Gram and I thought it would help break the ice if you dropped by to eat with us."

James was elated. "Really? That's wonderful."

"We'll see. I was going to try to rent an apartment for a month or so to give Gram and him a little more privacy but I haven't been able to find a thing." She made a comical face. "Max is going to be so frosted when he finds me living there again."

Taking a moment to think, James smiled

and said, "Why don't you move into the parsonage?"

Before he could explain more fully, Lillie gasped. "What?"

He waved his hands, palms out, in a gesture of innocence and denial. "No, no. I didn't mean it like that. I'll sleep at the church. It has a kitchen and all the other facilities I'd need. Besides, I eat most of my meals right here. You'd have the whole house to yourself for as long as you like."

"I don't think that's such a good idea."

"Why not? It would all be open and above board."

"To you and me, maybe," she said. "Not to the rest of the town."

"Okay. Whatever you say. I was only trying to help."

"Speaking of helping," she said, "I just remembered something." Reaching into her pocket, she withdrew a small white envelope. "I found this on the floor when I opened up this morning. It must have been slipped under the front door before I got here. It's addressed to you. See?"

"To me?" He accepted the envelope, then frowned as he recognized the handwriting.

"Aren't you going to open it?"

James slipped it into his jacket pocket. "Later."

"Okay. Whatever."

He could tell she was put off by his secrecy. Still, he didn't want to involve her if the letter was from the disturbing source he suspected it was.

"I have to keep my work separate from my personal life," he said, forcing a smile. "If you and I are going to become a couple, you need to understand that, Lillie. It's not that I don't want to share things with you. It's simply the way it has to be."

"You're right. I'm sorry."

"No apology necessary," he replied, standing and leaning over the counter toward her. To his relief, she, too, leaned closer.

She closed her eyes.

And he kissed her. Right there, in front of the whole breakfast crowd.

When he bid her goodbye and headed for the door, he was grinning. As he zigzagged past the occupied tables, three of his male parishioners held up their hands and gave him high fives!

* * *

Darla Sue was standing at the grill, smiling, as Lillie entered the kitchen. "You saw?"

"I did. You sure about this, girl?"

Lillie's lips still tingled and she couldn't stop grinning from ear to ear. "No. But I'm willing to give it a try."

"Fair enough. You do know about his past, don't you?"

"What do you mean? That he was married before?"

The older woman sobered. "That, and his almost goin' to jail for some kind of stock swindle."

"That was his partners' doing, not his," Lillie insisted.

"So he says. I've heard otherwise a time or two."

"From who?"

"Can't say. You just be careful. As they say, where there's smoke, there's fire. That's why I quit going to Front Porch Christian in the first place."

"You've been going lately," Lillie reminded her.

"Because of you, mostly. And I'm not

sayin' the preacher's a crook. He seems fine. I'm just tellin' you to look before you leap, that's all."

Lillie huffed quietly. There was no doubt that she'd already leaped, in her heart and mind at least. She refused to even consider the possibility that James, her James, was anything but the honest, sincere man he seemed to be.

It suddenly occurred to her that if she could get her grandmother to reveal the source of the gossip about him, she might have a clue to the identity of the man and woman she'd overheard talking that Sunday morning during the service.

"I'm going to need more than a few rumors to change my mind about James," Lillie said flatly. "If you can't tell me more, I'm not even going to consider giving him up." Pausing, she waited to see what her grandmother was going to do.

"Well," Darla Sue drawled, "if you insist. I heard it from Bobby Dean's mama, Neva."

"And you believed it? You know how that woman loves to stir up trouble."

"I know she can be an awful pill some-times but that doesn't mean she's always wrong. George Caldwell, that fella she married, knows all about it, firsthand. He was one of the people who lost a passel of money."

Aha! Now things were starting to make sense. Although Lillie didn't know why Bobby Dean's mother and her new husband would have been in the Front Porch congregation in the first place, it was highly possible that they had been the unknown voices in the pew behind her. It certainly explained their reference to her past relationships and Bobby Dean's supposedly broken heart.

She whipped off her apron and threw it down on a side counter in the kitchen as she said, "I have to leave for a few minutes. Ask Helen to watch my tables?"

Before Darla Sue could object, Lillie had darted out the back door and was on her way to the church to tell James what she'd learned. Once he had more facts, he'd be in a far better position to handle the touchy situation.

Rounding the corner onto Third Street, she broke into a trot. James was going to be so pleased with her! She could hardly wait to tell him everything.

The letter Lillie had delivered to him had upset James more than the similar ones before it. He'd thought all the intimidation would end when the criminals who had been using the cave had been apprehended.

Now, he wondered if he'd been wrong. He supposed the newest note could have been left before all the crooks had been arrested but he doubted it. Not only were the threats continuing, they now involved Lillie by virtue of the way the latest letter had been delivered.

This had to stop. Clearly, it was time to turn all the evidence over to Caleb Frost and trust that he'd take the warning notes seriously.

James was holding the most recent letter in one hand and reaching for the telephone on his desk with the other when he heard the outer door slamming and footsteps hurrying down the hall.

Lillie burst through the door and bypassed his secretary as if she weren't sitting there.

That brought Mary June to her feet. "Whoa. Hold on!"

James waved her off. "It's okay. I'll handle this." He took Lillie's arm and ushered her inside. "What's wrong? Has something happened to Miss Darla Sue?"

"No, no. She's fine."

"Then what…"

"I know who it is," Lillie blurted. "At least I think I do."

He pushed the office door closed behind her to keep their conversation a little more private. "Who what is? What are you talking about?"

"The folks I heard talking behind me that Sunday morning. Remember? I told you all about it, right after it happened."

His grip tightened on the note he still held. "I remember. Who do you think it was?"

"Bobby Dean's mother and her new husband, George Caldwell. It all fits. Gram says she heard that George lost money in the investment scam you told me about."

"That doesn't mean it was them talking."

"Yes, it does." Lillie's cheeks warmed noticeably. "At least I think so. I didn't tell you everything they said."

He frowned. "You didn't?"

"No. The woman was also complaining that I had ruined her son's life. You know I used to date Bobby Dean when we were in high school. I can't think of anybody else it could have been but Neva and George Caldwell."

James reached into the center drawer of his desk and gathered up the other notes he'd received. "I see. All right. I'll look up their address and go see them."

He noticed her attention focusing on the letters he held.

"What are all those?" Lillie asked.

"Nothing. I'll handle it."

"You don't trust me?"

James shook his head, looked into her eyes and tried to will her to understand. "It's not that, Lillie. I told you before, there are many things a pastor can't share with anyone. That's just the way it is. I'm sorry."

She took a step backward. "Right. Okay. I get it."

As she turned, jerked open the office door and stalked out, James was convinced she didn't begin to comprehend his dilemma. As much as he would have liked to disclose his concerns, when a subject involved his work for the church, he just could not. He would not. It wasn't ethical.

"So, where did you run off to?" Darla Sue asked.

"No place." Lillie wasn't keen on revealing her dash to tell James everything she'd learned, especially not after the way he'd summarily shut her out. It was embarrassing.

Her grandmother huffed. "Phooey. You lit out of here like your shoes were on fire. Don't you lie to me, girl."

Unshed tears filled Lillie's eyes. "I'm sorry, Gram. You're right. I went over to Front Porch Christian to let Brother James know who might be mad at him."

"Why?"

"Beats me. It seemed like the right thing to do at the time."

"And you don't think so now?"

"I don't know what to think." She shrugged and busied herself tearing lettuce into tiny shreds so she wouldn't have to look directly at her grandmother.

"We'll have enough dinner salads for an army if you don't quit doing that," Darla Sue said wryly. "What happened? Did you find out your preacher friend is a crook after all?"

Lillie whirled. "No! Nothing like that. It's just that I'm beginning to see that I'm not cut out to be a pastor's wife—or even his girl-friend—and I don't like the idea of giving up my dreams."

"Are you sure you have to?"

Sadly, Lillie nodded. "I'm sure. I know I can't be the kind of saintly, understanding, spiritually strong wife James needs. Not even close. And I can't honestly lead him on. It wouldn't be fair."

"Don't you think you may be making more of this whole thing than it deserves? After all, nothing says he's earnest about courting you."

"Actually, that's exactly what James *did* say. He's asked to date me. For real." Her cheeks warmed. "We were kind of pretend-ing, before."

"I figured as much. So, when did it turn serious?"

"A while ago. I don't think either of us realized how emotionally attached we were becoming until I got lost in the woods and he rescued me."

"Did your thankfulness wear off this fast?"

"No, no. I still think he's the most wonderful man I've ever met. That's why I can't consider saddling him with a wife like me. I get mad every time he clams up and doesn't tell me what he's doing. I can't help myself. And I can't begin to be as forgiving as he is, either. Take Grandpa Max, for instance. I'm dreading having to see him again."

"Humph. Well, you'd better plan on hiding in your room, then, because in case you've forgotten, we're having both Max and Brother James for supper tomorrow night."

Lillie gasped. "I'd totally put that out of my mind." Her eyes widened as she stared at her grandmother. "Do you think I could uninvite James?"

"Nope. What's done is done. You and I will just have to stick together and support each other while those two men are in the house."

"Oh," Lillie moaned. "I think I'm getting a headache."

Darla Sue snorted derisively. "Honey,

when you fall for a man, good or bad, you can count on having plenty of those."

James was disappointed. He'd telephoned the Caldwell house to ask if he might visit and had been turned down flat. He assumed that the woman he'd spoken to had been Bobby Dean's mother, although he wasn't positive. Her antagonistic attitude fit all the negative things he'd heard about her, however, so he assumed it was she who had answered the phone and had become so unfriendly as soon as he'd identified himself.

If Lillie was correct about the origin of the threatening letters, James didn't want to involve the sheriff. Not yet. There was no need making everything public if Caldwell was simply blowing off steam.

Therefore, James felt he must somehow arrange to speak with the man in person and clear the air.

He cruised in the direction of Serenity as he pondered what he'd say—what he should say—when and if he met with his supposed antagonist. There was no way to predict how he would be received if he showed up, uninvited, at the man's home, but he couldn't see any other practical alternative.

The old part of Serenity was laid out in a grid, very similar to Gumption's plan, which made it easier to find his way. Numbered streets ran east and west. He was looking for an address on Sixth.

He slowed, wheeled to the curb in front of a modest 1950s ranch-style home and checked his notes. This had to be the right house. And it appeared that the residents were home. A middle-aged, rather portly woman was kneeling, working in the flower beds on one side of the house. On the opposite side, a gray-haired man of about sixty was maneuvering a gas-powered lawn mower out of the garage.

James parked and headed for him. Judging by the way the man immédiately froze and stared, he figured he'd found George Caldwell. In seconds he was positive.

"Mr. Caldwell?"

"What if I am?"

"I'm Brother Warner from Front Porch Christian Church." James offered his hand. The man made no move to take it.

"I know who you are."

"Good. Then perhaps we can talk about your concerns."

"Don't know what you mean." Caldwell started to push the lawn mower ahead.

James stood his ground and blocked the path.

"I think you do." He reached into his jacket pocket and withdrew one of the threatening notes.

Judging by the look on the other man's face, James was certain he knew exactly what was written on the folded paper. When he didn't own up to it right away, James said, "If I've done anything you feel is wrong, I'd like you to tell me what it was so I can ask your forgiveness."

"Forgiveness? Bah! There are some things that are way beyond that, Preacher."

"For us humans, maybe," James said, working to keep his tone even and uncritical. "But God can work things out if we let Him."

"Can He bring back the fortune you stole from me?"

"Well, He hasn't returned the money I lost by making the same investments you did. But He has given me something much more valuable."

"Like what?" The man's face was twisted in a leer.

"Peace. And an assurance of my place in His family."

"You expect me to believe that you lost money, too? What do you take me for?"

"An unhappy man who thinks bearing a grudge is his only recourse," James ventured. "I do understand how you feel. I was angry at my ex-wife and my former partners for far too long. All that got me was an ulcer."

Caldwell rubbed his own stomach. "I know what that's like, believe you me."

"I do believe you," James said with evident empathy. "Nursing a grudge can actually make a person sick. It did me." He began nodding to mirror the other man's subconscious reaction. "I'm not asking you to forget what happened. I only wanted to tell you that I am truly sorry."

George's bushy gray eyebrow arched. "Did you really take a bath along with the rest of us?"

"Yes," James assured him. "I was bank-rupted, too. At the time, it seemed like the end of the world, but I don't complain anymore. If I hadn't lost everything, I might never have gotten squared away with God. And I know I wouldn't be living here in the Ozarks and enjoying the second chance I've been given." He paused to allow the other man an opportunity to respond.

"I—I didn't know you lost money, too," Caldwell finally said. "Guess it never occurred to me."

"I really didn't know what was going on until it was too late for all of us," James said. "If there had been any way I could have reimbursed the other investors out of my own pocket, I would have."

"I'm beginning to think you would."

"That's all I ask." James again offered to shake hands and this time Caldwell obliged. "Do you want your letters back?" James asked.

"Burn 'em. Burn 'em and forget 'em."

James began to grin as he pumped the other man's hand. "Consider it done. Will I see you and Mrs. Caldwell this Sunday in church?"

"You might," George said. "You just might. We don't usually go anywhere but we did drop in at your church a while back to check it out, to see if it was really you preaching. When Neva mentioned your name I had to see for myself if it was the same James Warner I'd known up north. Seemed too far-fetched for us to both wind up in the same corner of Arkansas."

"The Lord does work in mysterious ways," James said, still smiling. "I never cease to be amazed."

Chapter Fifteen

"I'm as nervous as my cats would be in a room full of pit bulls," Darla Sue said, patting her new hairdo and blinking at her reflection in the glass doors of the dish cupboard in the dining room.

Lillie chuckled wryly. "Me, too. Are you sure we should be making this dinner so formal? I mean, you and Max usually ate all your meals in the kitchen, even when I was little. Wouldn't that be more relaxing?"

"I don't particularly want that old fool to be relaxed," Darla Sue said. "And I'm not about to entertain the preacher in my kitchen. It's not seemly."

"Okay. This is your dinner party."

Lillie sighed as she rechecked the table

settings. The good china shone; the glasses sparkled and the silverware was perfectly aligned beside each plate. The napkins were ecru linen and matched the tablecloth, which was a far cry from the paper and plastic they usually used.

If she had thought it would help her avoid being too near James during the meal, Lillie would have opted for formal place cards, too. However, considering the fact that there were only going to be four for supper, it hardly mattered. Regardless of where he decided to sit, he was going to wind up too close.

She checked her watch and noted that it was nearly 6:00 p.m. Having worked all morning, she'd normally have been barefoot and dressed in something far more casual by this time of day. Instead, she was wearing her favorite embroidered georgette blouse, a slim dark skirt and low heels. She hadn't been this dressed up in a long, long time.

It's only because that's what Gram wanted, Lillie told herself.

She huffed with disgust. She might get away with blaming Darla Sue for all the folderol as far as James and Max were concerned but in her heart she knew better. There hadn't been one second while she was dressing and fixing her hair that she hadn't been thinking of the impression she'd be making on James when he saw her. And that was so wrong.

She was about to tell her grandmother about her growing misgivings when there was a knock on the back door. One look at Darla Sue's stunned expression told Lillie she'd better be the one to volunteer to answer the door.

Her heels clicked on the kitchen floor as she crossed the worn linoleum. Through the window at the top of the door she could see that their guest was not James.

She steeled herself, forced a smile that she hoped wasn't too false looking and twisted the knob. "Hello, Grandpa Max."

If he was surprised to see her there he hid it well. "Hello, Lillie." He removed his navy-and-gold Florida souvenir baseball cap and held it in his hands. "Can I come in? Your grandma's expectin' me."

"I know." She stood back to grant him access.

He stepped inside tentatively, not at all

like the swaggering, forthright man she remembered him to be.

"She's in the dining room," Lillie said.

"Will you come with me?" He was worrying the cap with gnarled fingers.

"Of course. That's why I'm here."

Max managed a slight smile. "To keep her from conking me with a skillet, the way Annabelle did those soldiers?"

"Something like that." In spite of the fact that Lillie was righteously angry with him because of the way he'd treated her grandmother, she couldn't help feeling a bit sorry for him, too.

About to turn away from the door, she heard the roar of an approaching Harley.

Apparently Max did, too, because he blanched. "Don't tell me the preacher's coming, too?"

"He certainly is. Gram invited him to eat with us," Lillie said. She pulled a face in response to the one Max was displaying. "We thought it would be best if there was a disinterested third party here when you and Gram discussed your plans."

He nodded. "It's no more than I deserve. How is your grandma, anyway?"

"Just peachy, no thanks to you," Lillie said. "How could you do such a thing?"

"I had my reasons."

"Oh, I'm sure you think you did. And maybe she'll forgive you. I don't know. All I'm sure of is that I won't."

"Fair enough," Max said softly. "All I really care about is making up with my darlin' Darla."

Outside, the motorcycle cruised to a stop and the engine quieted. Lillie waited by the open door with her grandfather until James appeared.

"Hi," he said enthusiastically. He grabbed Max's hand and pumped it as if he were greeting a long-lost buddy. "Max! How are you?"

"Fair to middling," the older man said. "You here to tell me I'm goin' to you-know-where in a handbasket, too?"

James glanced at Lillie for a split second. "Nope. That's between you and God and your wife. I'm just glad you decided to come home."

"Yeah. Me, too."

Lillie stood back and gestured for the others to precede her. "Shall we go in to supper? Grandma's got everything arranged on the sideboard, including the pot roast. She started supper in a Crock-Pot early this morning so it would be cooked and ready when we got home from work."

"I love pot roast," James said. He clapped Max on the back. "Come on. If it tastes as good as it smells, we're in for a real treat."

Lillie could tell that her grandfather was hesitant and she was glad to see James taking charge of the situation. She supposed, since it had been difficult for her to swallow her pride and come home, this must be even harder for Max. Well, good. If any man deserved to suffer and struggle with a guilty conscience, it was that man. What he had done was terrible. Unconscionable. Totally beyond redemption.

She couldn't make out what her grandfather mumbled as he passed through the doorway into the dining room but she did hear James's reply.

When he said, "It's not for us to judge," she felt as if God had reached down and tapped her on the shoulder to get her full attention and make His point.

See? she insisted silently. *See? I was right.*

*I am totally unsuited to become a pastor's
wife. If I were any less spiritual I'd be on a
par with Max!*

That unacceptable notion was almost
enough to turn her stomach. Being this close
to James and knowing she'd have to tell him
how she felt very soon, she wondered if
she'd be able to choke down much supper,
no matter how tasty it was. Somehow, she
doubted it.

Darla Sue had greeted her wandering
husband with reserve and had permitted him
to kiss her on the cheek but James could see
she was teetering on the brink of tears, while
Lillie kept looking from her grandmother to
her grandfather and fuming. The conflict
wasn't as bad as that of Daniel in the lion's
den but James couldn't help making the
comparison. He felt as if one wrong word
would result in the whole situation blowing
up in their faces.

He'd been praying silently while making
small talk. Now that they'd eaten and had a
chance to calm down a bit, he decided it was
time to ask a few pointed questions.

Folding his napkin and placing it next to

his plate, he looked at Max. "So, tell us. What made you decide to finally come home?"

The older man coughed. His blue eyes grew misty. "Got lonesome, I reckon."

Lillie's blurted "Ha!" brought a stern look from James.

He turned back to the old man with a gently spoken "Go on."

"I just wanted to see my Darla Sue again. I missed her something fierce."

James looked to her and smiled slightly to encourage her to reply.

"If you missed me," she said with a catch in her voice, "why did you leave in the first place?"

Somber, Max shook his head. "I've tried to explain how I felt for years. You never would listen. You and I, we don't have a lot of time left. I wanted to travel, to see the country while we were still able to enjoy it. But all you ever wanted to do was work."

"My café helped support us both for years," she snapped back. "Especially after you retired from the power company."

"Yes, it did. And I was always grateful. But I thought there ought to be more to life than just sittin' on the porch and rockin' till we keeled over. I thought…"

James urged him to continue. "You thought what, Max?"

"I thought…" He swallowed hard, his Adam's apple bobbing. "I thought it would be fun to travel, even if Darla Sue wouldn't go with me." He shook his head. "But I was wrong. I was miserable, worrying about her and wishing she was there to enjoy it all, too."

"Horse feathers!" the older woman said. "You had plenty of company."

"But I didn't have *you*." Max reached for his wife's hand and she let him take it, hold it. "You were always the only girl for me."

"You're an old fool," she said with a catch in her voice.

"I know. The question is, can you put up with me for another fifty years or so?"

"I suppose I might try."

James could have leaped up and cheered. Yes, they had a long way to go in working out a lasting reconciliation, but this was an excellent first step, one he'd hardly dared imagine would occur so easily.

His gaze met Lillie's. Teary-eyed, she

seemed on the verge of weeping. It was his fondest hope that her emotions were those of gladness.

Then, sadly, he saw her features harden, her jaw muscles clench, and he knew otherwise.

Lillie had volunteered to clean up the kitchen rather than remain in the room with her grandparents. They were acting like teenagers in the throes of their first crush and the sight upset her greatly.

She was standing at the sink, scraping table scraps into the cat's food dishes, when James joined her.

"Shall I put the leftover roast in the refrigerator?" he asked. "I know better than to leave it on the table where the cats can steal it."

"That's fine. I think there's room."

When he came up behind her and lightly touched her arm, she startled. He laughed quietly. "I know how you feel. I'm pretty jumpy myself. But I do think your grandparents will be okay, don't you?"

"Nobody cares what I think. If they did, Gram would have thrown Max out on his ear the minute he showed his face in this house. He doesn't deserve her forgiveness."

"No, he doesn't. None of us deserves God's grace, either, but that doesn't mean He won't grant it if we're penitent."

She whirled. "See what I mean? That's a perfect example."

"Of what?" James's brow furrowed.

"Of why you and I will never be right for each other. We don't think the same way. Not even close. You're so spiritual it makes me feel like something you find in the mud under a rock."

"Don't be ridiculous." He tried to take her hand, but she jerked it away.

"*You're* the one who's being ridiculous," Lillie said, trying to control the rising volume of her voice and failing. "You think that just because we happen to get along pretty well, we're suited for each other. Well, we're not. My mother didn't realize how right she was when she said I was emotionally unstable."

"What are you talking about?"

"Me. Inside." After wiping her hands on a towel, she tapped an index finger in the center of her sternum. "I can't be the partner you need or the woman you think I am. I wish I could."

James grasped her upper arms and held her fast so she had no choice but to look at him. "Do you think that I don't struggle, that I don't have to work at it every single day? Do you think my thoughts are so pure that I'm above you? Well, I'm not. I'm human, too, Lillie. We all are. The difference is, believers have God's help to get us through difficulties and temptations, if we'll only accept it."

"That doesn't change a thing," she insisted, biting her lower lip until it hurt.

"It can."

She didn't want to look into his eyes, to see the compassion and love reflected there, but she could not make herself avert her gaze. Trembling, speechless, she merely shook her head.

It wasn't going to do him any good to keep preaching to her, she vowed. She wasn't going to listen. He might be right about some things but she knew he was wrong this time. She, Lillie Rose Iris Daisy Delaney, was not anywhere near good enough for him. Fortunately, she loved him enough to put his interests first and keep telling him so, as often as necessary, until he accepted it. ¯

Thankfully, she was able to hold back her tears until James walked silently away and left her feeling more miserable than she had in her whole life.

Lillie had had no intention of attending Front Porch Christian the following Sunday—or any other time, for that matter. Unfortunately, her grandparents had wanted her to accompany them and she was eventually persuaded by Darla Sue's earnest, repeated pleas.

"We want you with us. Please say you'll go?" the older woman had urged.

"I don't know why you think you need my company anymore," Lillie had replied. "Aren't you and Grandpa getting along okay?"

"Yes. But Max is worried about what folks will say and I thought, if you were with us, it would seem like you supported our decision to reconcile."

"I support *you*," Lillie had said. "That's the best I can do. Sorry."

"That's good enough, for now." Darla Sue had been grinning as she'd spoken.

Which was why Lillie was now seated next to her grandparents in a rear pew of Front Porch Christian. As usual, the sanctuary was filled almost to overflowing.

She leaned closer to Darla Sue to say "If it gets any more crowded in here we'll be sitting on each other's laps."

The older woman giggled behind her hand. "Want me to move over and sit on Max's so you'll have more room?"

"Gram! Shame on you. And in church, too!"

"Oh, chill out, girl. I was only joking. Besides, we're married."

"Chill out?" Lillie's eyebrows arched dramatically. "Where did that kind of slang come from?"

"I've decided I've been too stuffy," she answered. "Max was right. I need to have more fun. With him. And as soon as you're ready to take over DD's full-time, we're going to start to travel, like he wants."

"Is it what you want?" Lillie asked in a whisper.

"Yes. Oh, I know it'll be hard for me to let go at first but I'll adjust. You just watch. We're going to have a blast. It'll be like the second honeymoon we never got around to taking."

"A second honeymoon? When were you planning to do that?"

"Oh, years and years ago. It's not important. Forget I mentioned it," she said as she reached for her husband's hand and entwined her fingers with his.

Lillie suddenly suspected that she knew exactly when they had been going to take that trip. "It was about the time I came to live with you, wasn't it? That's why you never got to go."

"It doesn't matter now," Darla Sue said sweetly. "All that counts is that we've been given another chance and we're going to take advantage of it. I wish you could be happier for us, honey."

"I am happy for you. Honest, I am," Lillie said, trying to hide the tears welling in her eyes. No wonder Max had seemed so disgruntled when she'd come to live with them. Now that she knew the whole story, Lillie wasn't surprised that he'd been upset, especially since his special plans had been thwarted so completely.

Ashamed of her prior animosity, she was

about to lean past Darla Sue and try to find the proper words to apologize to Max when the choir entered and the service began, postponing her chance to speak with him.

As usual, the sight of James taking his place in the front of the sanctuary made Lillie's pulse jump. She swallowed hard to choke back her turbulent feelings.

Although she went through the motions and sang the familiar opening hymns with the rest of the congregation, she wasn't really paying attention. Instead, her mind was racing, her thoughts spinning.

She had been an innocent child caught up in adult divisiveness when she'd been sent to live with her grandparents. Nevertheless, she had caused far more strife between them than she'd ever imagined. Under those circumstances it was a wonder that either of them had accepted her, let alone loved her the way Darla Sue had.

She reached to pat her grandmother's thin hand as Brother James stepped forward to begin his sermon.

He scanned the congregation. Then, as his gaze found Lillie's, he nodded and appeared to relax.

"I have a little experiment I'd like you all to help me with," he said with a smile. "I've put some polished stones in the racks for the hymnals on the back of each pew. I'll wait while you look for them."

Lillie reached forward and found a smooth, colored rock about the size of a large grape. She'd seen similar ones for sale by the pound in lapidary and craft shops. Hers was pretty, with swirls of yellow and black. Darla had found a greenish one.

"Here's mine." James displayed a larger rock with more acute angles, then placed it in front of him on the leading edge of the lectern where everyone could easily see it. "I want you to turn to the Book of John, chapter eight."

He began to read. Anticipating the scripture's teaching because she recognized it, Lillie felt tears start to cloud her vision.

When James concluded by quoting, "'He that is without sin among you, let him cast the first stone,'" Lillie realized he was speaking directly to her. This was what he'd been trying to say when he'd explained his feelings in her grandmother's kitchen! The message wasn't only for her, either. It pertained to everyone. Could she accept such a plain truth? Would it change anything if she did?

James continued to speak and illustrate his text while Lillie's mind forged ahead. Her misgivings couldn't be this simple. Nothing was that cut-and-dried. Yet, in the deepest reaches of her soul, she was beginning to sense a peace she had not experienced before.

"In conclusion," James said, "I'd like to invite you to either keep your stones as a reminder of this message, or throw them at me if you think you're sinless." He paused and smiled. "I'll wait."

The smile broadened to a grin as not a single stone flew in any direction. "Good. I see we understand each other. Now, if you'd like to start over the way the woman in this scripture did, I invite you to come forward and do so as the choir sings our closing hymn."

If Lillie had not been seated next to the aisle, she might have been able to delay long enough to talk herself out of making a move. As it was, her easy access to the long, carpeted center aisle was an incentive she couldn't defy.

With no more than a few seconds' pause she stepped forward and headed for James. By the time she reached him, she was practically running.

Obviously touched, he took her hand and felt the polished stone she still held in it. "I won't be throwing that at you or anyone else," he said quietly, just for her ears. "Can you understand that, Lillie?"

She nodded. Tears were streaming down her cheeks. "You have every right to," she stammered. "I was so wrong about Max. About everything."

"There are no rules that say we have to be right all the time," James said. "Only that we have to try our best to live as the Bible teaches. It's not about keeping rules, Lillie. It's about having an open mind and a forgiving, loving heart. You have that. You just weren't ready to acknowledge it."

"I—I'm so sorry," she said.

"Don't be sorry. Just tell me you'll give yourself another chance. Give God another chance to show you His way and lead you through life."

Again she nodded, emboldened by the strength of purpose and inner calm she had begun to sense. "Will you give me another chance, too?" she asked.

James clasped her hands in both of his and nodded, his eyes misty, his smile so beautiful it took Lillie's breath away.

When he said, "I never stopped," it was all she could do to contain her joy.

Grinning, she sniffled and blinked back more tears, tears of immense relief and gladness. There would have to be more depth to their relationship than there was at present, she knew, yet she also knew, without a doubt, that they did have a future together.

Would she be the perfect preacher's wife? Probably not. But she was going to give it her best. Beyond that, it was all up to God.

Now that she was seeing things more clearly, she realized it always had been.

Epilogue

Logan Malloy had gladly come over from Serenity to Gumption to perform the marriage ceremony uniting James Robert Warner and Lillie Rose Iris Daisy Delaney in holy matrimony.

Lillie would have scheduled the nuptials sooner, but she'd wanted to wait until her grandparents got back from their extended Mediterranean cruise. She'd received postcards regularly and an occasional phone call, but she'd still missed them something awful—even Max.

Front Porch Christian's building project had progressed nicely, although the new sanctuary was still in the framing stage. Lillie had insisted that she and James be married on the outlying church property regardless of the unfinished state of the structure, so the ladies' society had decorated some of the standing open beams with greenery and flowers to resemble an old-fashioned brush arbor.

Against the gold-and-red-and-orange backdrop of the forest in its full autumn glory, Lillie thought the makeshift arbor was more beautiful than any fancy chapel would have been. Hers was to be the first wedding held there and she wouldn't have cared if the only canopy they'd had over them was God's blue sky.

Mary June had acted as wedding planner and caterer, while Chancy Collins was her matron of honor.

"And you're sure he's the one?" Chancy asked as she adjusted Lillie's veil.

Lillie nodded. "Yes. Positive."

"I think so, too. See? Smart women who agree. How can you doubt?"

Lillie gave her a quick hug. "I'm not doubting James. I'm just hoping I won't trip or something."

"You'll be fine. And I'll be close by to catch you in case you do and James misses."

She giggled. "by the looks of it, I'd say he can handle just about anything—even *you!*"

"Thanks—I think."

A portable keyboard had been set up next to the temporary power pole on the church property and the organist was warming up for Lillie's wedding by playing a series of uplifting praise songs.

Lillie couldn't stop grinning so widely her cheeks hurt. She blinked back tears of joy and shaded her eyes against the bright fall sun.

Mary June appeared, a handkerchief in one hand and the bride's bouquet in the other. "Are you ladies ready?"

"I think so." Lillie straightened the lacy white skirt of her gown and accepted her bouquet of asters and baby's breath. "Are you okay? You look kind of pale."

Mary June gave a nervous laugh. "Me? I'm as nervous as a mama seeing her own son get married."

"You should be. James has often said he thinks of you as his family."

"I wish his mama and daddy had lived long enough to see him this happy." Mary June sniffled. "Is your mother here?"

"Yes. And my father, too," Lillie said.

"It's all patched up between them and you?"

Lillie smiled and nodded. "As patched up as the good Lord can make it and that's good enough for me."

She stepped out from behind a lattice work screen and looked toward the altar where James and Brother Logan waited. Her gaze met James's and held it.

He smiled.

Trembling, Lillie took a deep breath.

The notes of the wedding march began to swell in the crisp fall air. A faint breeze fluttered the colorful leaves, making the forest seem as if it were sighing and rejoicing in concert with the happy couple.

Lillie's veil lifted ever so slightly and brushed against her rosy cheeks as she prepared to follow Chancy down the makeshift aisle.

Bravely, trusting God, she began to take the first steps that would carry her to James's side. The past was gone and forgotten. The future was ahead. She could hardly wait to see what marvelous blessings it held.

Dear Reader,

In this story, both Lillie and James decide to change careers in midlife. I did the same thing. That doesn't mean my original choices were wrong, only that it was time to move on, to try something new, to spread my wings and follow the Lord's leading. Change can be scary. And mistakes are always possible no matter how hard we try to avoid them, which is why major changes in our lives need a lot of prior prayer and careful consideration.

My prayer for all of you is that you will find the happiness, fulfillment and contentment we all seek. I have. And I thank God every day for the wonderful life He has given me.

I love to hear from readers—by e-mail, VAL@ValerieHansen.com, or at P.O. Box 13, Glencoe, AR, 72539. I'll do my best to answer as soon as I can. Drop by my Web site, www.ValerieHansen.com, for the latest news on my current and upcoming books.

Blessings,

Valerie Hansen

QUESTIONS FOR DISCUSSION

1. This book is about change. Have you ever thought of making major changes in your life? If you did make the changes, what were they?

2. Lillie is positive she wants to remain single. Have you ever been sure of something important and later decided you were wrong? Why or why not?

3. James has been given a second chance and has begun a new career. Have you ever been in a similar situation and let the chance slip away?

4. The small-town atmosphere shapes the lives of everyone in Gumption, just as it did in my other fictional town of Serenity. Do you see this closeness as an asset or a drawback? Why or why not?

5. Unseen forces seem to be working against the expansion of Front Porch Christian Church. Have you ever been in

a church that was growing rapidly and you wished it was not? It's a normal human reaction to want things to stay the same, but is it fair?

6.   Memories may be influencing Lillie's current choices. Do you believe God is able to mend broken hearts and minds? Have you seen it happen? (I have!)

7.   Lillie's parents and grandparents have had stormy marriages. Do you think that dooms Lillie to follow in their footsteps? Who—or what—will help her overcome her fears?

8.   If Lillie turns her heart over to the Lord, can she expect healing? Will that healing necessarily occur the way she thinks it will? Might God, in His greater wisdom, have something even better planned for her?

9.   Sometimes we tend to blame ourselves when things don't go according to our plans. If Lillie's grandparents

had not reconciled, would it have been her fault? Why not?

10. The scripture I chose for this story is found in Romans 12:18. It says we should live peaceably with everyone *as much as it depends on us*. If Lillie's parents or the man who was holding a grudge against James had refused to reconsider no matter what, would that have been James's or Lillie's problem? Why did they need to do their best and leave the results up to God?

HEARTWARMING INSPIRATIONAL ROMANCE

Contemporary,
inspirational romances
with Christian characters
facing the challenges
of life and love
in today's world.

**NOW AVAILABLE IN REGULAR
AND LARGER-PRINT FORMATS.**

**Steeple
Hill®**

For exciting stories that reflect traditional values,
visit:
www.SteepleHill.com

LIGEN07R

Love Inspired®
SUSPENSE
RIVETING INSPIRATIONAL ROMANCE

Watch for our new series of
edge-of-your-seat suspense novels.
These contemporary tales
of intrigue and romance
feature Christian characters
facing challenges to their faith...
and their lives!

Steeple
Hill®

Visit:
www.SteepleHill.com

LISUSDIR07R